THE PLYMOUTH PAPERS

BEING

THE HISTORY OF STEPHEN HOPKINS,

HIS SON GILES, CATHERINE WHELDEN,

CALEB HOPKINS AND DIVERS OTHERS,

BOTHE ENGLISH AND INDIAN,

WHO INHABITED THE COLONY

CALLED PLYMOUTH

IN THE 1600'S

CLIFTON SNIDER

THE PLYMOUTH PAPERS

BEING

THE HISTORY OF STEPHEN HOPKINS,

HIS SON GILES, CATHERINE WHELDEN,

CALEB HOPKINS AND DIVERS OTHERS,

BOTHE ENGLISH AND INDIAN,

WHO INHABITED THE COLONY

CALLED PLYMOUTH

IN THE 1600'S

CLIFTON SNIDER

SPOUT HILL PRESS

First Edition
February 2014
Copyright ©2014 by Clifton Snider.

www.spouthillpress.com
Seal Beach, California

Cover art and design by Ann Brantingham
Author photo by Deborah Snider

ISBN 13: 978-0615956916
ISBN 10: 0615956912

For Mario Hernandez
& All Those Who Paved the Way

TABLE OF CONTENTS

CHAPTER ONE
DISCOVERY OF THE PAPERS
BY CALEB TAYLOR AND THE HISTORY
OF STEPHEN HOPKINS ON THE SEA VENTURE,
THE HORRENDOUS TEMPEST THAT CAUSED IT
TO SHIPWRECK IN THE BERMUDAS, HIS RETURN
TO ENGLAND, THE VOYAGE ON THE MAYFLOWER,
ITS LANDING AT CAPE COD, ETC.

20 JANUARY 1864, BOSTON, MASSACHUSETTS

I F THE TITLE of my book seems a bit grand, it is only because I think my subject grand, and I want to follow traditions of seventeenth-century publishers. After all, these Plymouth Papers come from that era. Although I own a small publishing firm in Boston, I am also an amateur historian and a devoted follower of modern literature as well. So you see, dear reader, I am not unfamiliar with the policies and practices of my industry, past and present.

Let me introduce myself. I am Caleb Taylor, a descendant on my mother's side from those people who today are called "Pilgrims," and I have long tossed around the idea of writing a little history of my own following the lives of my ancestors, who descend from Stephen Hopkins, the only *Mayflower* passenger, other than perhaps the master and members of his crew, who had been to the New World before the sailing of the *Mayflower*.

Only last Christmas did the topic of my proposed history come up when I and my younger brother, James, his wife, Isabel, and their two young boys journeyed by train, then coach and four, to my Aunt Huldah's house in Eastham

9

on Cape Cod to celebrate the holiday. Our sister, Sarah, had married and moved to Chicago. Worries about the war and the winter weather, always severe on the Cape but also in Chicago, prevented her and her family from coming. She telegraphed to give us the news. I myself have no other family. As a young man in my twenties, I was engaged to marry Martha, the most wonderful of young ladies, but she died of consumption. After that, nobody asked why I did not wed another. She was the one love of my life.

After we had dined and exchanged our gifts, James asked me if I were still planning to write my history.

"I have given thought to it," I replied. This was only half true. I hadn't really thought of it in months. My business was doing so well, despite the war, I had to hire an assistant and one extra worker. We did all the editing and typesetting ourselves, you see. I had started as a newspaper reporter and quickly began writing columns advocating the abolition of slavery. That led to a wealthy Boston merchant's suggestion that I set up my own press and print pamphlets, with his financial support. Soon we were making a profit and that allowed me to begin publishing books.

"Will I be in it?" said Silas, my thirteen-year-old nephew.

"Well, I don't know. I expect you might--whenever I get around to writing it."

"Caleb, you aren't going to bring up all those horrid old rumors, I hope," said Aunt Huldah. She was the last surviving member of her generation and, to the dismay of the entire family, had been converted from the Congregational Church to one of those radical new Christian sects in a camp meeting at Eastham, where she had lived all her life, even after her husband, a sea captain, had perished at sea ten years before. Or so everyone thought. He and his crew were never found. Nor was their ship.

"What rumors might those be?" I asked, knowing full well what she meant.

"Oh, you know, all that business about Indian blood and Stephen Hopkins being an insurrectionist in the South Seas."

"It was Bermuda, I believe. And he was a mutineer."

"Same thing, dear nephew. Surely there's no need to go over all that again."

"Well, I have to tell the truth, don't I, dear Aunt Huldah?"

"Caleb Taylor! You could skip over that part and still tell a truthful story."

"I'll think about it," I said. I really doubted I had time for such a project anyway.

"Hmm," she murmured. "Isabel, will you help me with the dessert?"

While Isabel and Aunt Huldah busied themselves in the kitchen, we male members of the family amused ourselves with the stereoscope I had given to Paul, the elder of James's sons, a boy of fifteen. The instrument had come with stereographs of Boston, New York, Washington, D. C., London, and Paris. It was really quite an amusing invention. I promised to have stereoscopic pictures made of the family in time for our next gathering which, I imagined, would be at Easter.

The women came back with a plum-filled pound cake and hot cider. Since her conversion, Huldah had stopped serving alcoholic drinks.

Despite her uncertain health, I had no clue that my aunt would be on her deathbed by the first week in the new year. She summoned me.

Her ghostly pallor reminded me of a character in a story by Edgar Allan Poe, that talented yet pathetic drunkard from the South. Aunt Huldah had already asked me, as the eldest of her nephews, since she had no surviving children of her own, to be her executor. "I have a request, dear nephew," she said in a tiny voice I could barely understand. "After I am gone, go to the attic. There you will find preserved in an old trunk some papers written by our ancestors from England and here in New England. I want you to destroy these papers."

"But my dear Aunt Huldah. Such papers are precisely what I need to write my history of the family."

"That is of no matter, dear Caleb. There are matters in our history which are unspeakable and should never be made known."

I could not imagine what such matters could be, unless they referred to the alleged Indian blood or the mutiny of Stephen Hopkins. Did she mean these, I asked her.

"Oh, no, not those. Truth be told, they are of no matter compared to the terrible sins of our forebears."

"Sins?" I could not imagine to what she referred.

"Yes, nephew. Sins. Sins of the flesh. Leviticus . . . the Apostle Paul," she gasped and fell into a deep slumber, a slumber from which she never awoke.

She died calmly in her sleep during the night. I, however, could not sleep, sitting by her bed and pondering her words. "Leviticus? The Apostle Paul?" I knew that Leviticus contains many outdated strictures and condemnations, and Paul was known to be both a champion of charity and an enemy of the body, he who declared, "It is good for a man not to touch a woman. . . . But if they cannot contain, let them marry: for it is better to marry than to burn." Is this what Aunt Huldah referred to? She had asked me to destroy the "papers," as she called them, but I had not promised I would. Still, if I could find any way to honor her deathbed wish, I was duty-bound to do it.

A FEW DAYS after her funeral, I summoned sufficient nerve to rummage through her attic. There I came upon some curious documents, documents that must have been the papers Aunt Huldah spoke of, preserved in an antique family chest--journals, letters, things of that sort--in a script that reminded me of the times nearly two hundred and fifty years ago when my ancestors came to this country.

Then it was no country at all, of course, but one which William Bradford, historian and long-time governor of Plymouth Colony, describes as "devoid of all civil inhabitants, where there are only savage and brutish men which range up and down, little otherwise than the wild beasts of the same." More than a little harsh on the Indians, wouldn't you say?

I was rather impressed to find among these papers my Christian name: Caleb. My mother had told me I was named after a favorite uncle, one of her late brothers. Now I wondered how he acquired *his* name, for here it was, scattered like purple shells on the shore, among the papers. I thought of Nathaniel Hawthorne, one of my favorite living writers. When I finish reading the papers, I believe I'll write to him about my findings. Perhaps they might contribute to his imaginative romances. Now I have the motivation to write my own factual memoir of the family and our so-called founding fathers. For the time being, I will let my assistant run my business.

THE LARGEST OF the documents is written by Giles Hopkins, son of Stephen and also a *Mayflower* passenger. This document, written in the form of a journal or memoir, ought to illuminate the beginnings of the English settlement of this country. Perhaps it will tell me what so scandalized Aunt Huldah. It will certainly help me write my history. Since Stephen Hopkins was his father, naturally Giles concentrates on him, so far as I can see. I have decided to transcribe the memoir into modern English, that is to render the spelling and punctuation modern. Also, following seventeenth-century style, I intend to indicate, as I make progress, the dates and locations Giles writes about so far as I can determine them, as well as the dates of my own commentaries. Perhaps instead of my own separate history, this manuscript by Giles and the other papers I have yet to examine will suffice. We shall see. Here begins the document:

1677, EASTHAM, CAPE COD, MASSACHUSETTS, THE MEMOIR OF GILES HOPKINS

To my dear wife, Catherine, and to our children, Mary, Stephen, Abigail, Deborah, Caleb, Joshua, and William, and their children and to divers persons who may wish to know the truth after my departure, I begin this testament to wash clean my conscience as to events I shall here inscribe regarding my behavior towards the natives of this land I have long called my own and over my behavior toward my brother, Caleb. I have long suffered over the question of my fidelity, or rather lack thereof, to Caleb and pondered as to

14

whether it has been that which a Christian, albeit not of the persuasion that now and since its inception dominates Plymouth Colony, ought to have perpetuated.

Although born of different mothers, and one could say almost to a different generation, I believe my brother Caleb and I were not unlike the renowned Biblical brothers, Cain and Abel or, better yet, Jacob and Esau. As such is the case, a history of the life of our father may and I believe ought to begin my narrative.

SUCH A NARRATIVE will not be difficult for Stephen Hopkins's eldest son, who, though cruelly separated from him for a period of years at a most tender age, listened to recitals of his history on numerous occasions during the idle hour or two after supper and before retirement. Indeed, during the first seven years of our life in Plymouth Plantation we all listened, the entire household: my sister, Constance, my stepmother Elizabeth and her children by my father: Damaris, Oceanus (he who was born at sea on the ship *Mayflower*), together with those born in the colony: Caleb and Deborah, who was only a babe in arms when the cattle were divided amongst the households in 1627. Lest I be accused of dissembling or being neglectful, I hasten to add that our household consisted also of two man servants, Edward Doty and Edward Leister. These will figure again in my narrative.

1609-13, GILES HOPKINS AS A CHILD IN LONDON AND THE ADVENTURES OF STEPHEN HOPKINS ON THE *SEA VENTURE*, FROM THE MEMOIR OF GILES HOPKINS
But to my father. To the world he appeared a learned man, stubborn, sometimes willful, but companionable and wise, particularly in his dealings with the people who

inhabited New England before it was New England. I can not speak for the other members of the aforementioned household, but to me he was the most wondrous of personages. That he was a handsome man with dark brown hair, deep brown, penetrating eyes, and a gait that inspired confidence or fear is attested by many others. You do not have to trust the word of his eldest son. In June 1609 when he left me, my mother Mary, never again to behold her face in this life, and my sisters Elizabeth and Constance, it was as if Heaven had turned its face against me. Though yet living at home with my family, I felt like Cain, expelled from the company of happy, congenial spirits. I felt as it were a sinner chained in the bonds of Hell. And when my dearest mother entered Heaven, my grief was insupportable. I observed the heads of the foul criminals on the pikes of the London Bridge and saw mine own pinioned there. My sisters perforce had to restrain me from flinging my body into the waters of the Thames. I was only five years of age. Our father presumed dead, Elizabeth, Constance, and I, orphaned in our tender years, had to provide for us two strange and hard men, Roberto Lyte and Thome Syms. These men did sell our shop of various liquors, spices, and kitchen herbs.

You may well imagine my astonishment, nay my ecstasy, if I may use a word associated with the Papist religion, when my father first appeared at our threshold about the year 1613, bearing wondrous and brave gifts, marvelous oranges and lemons, sugar cane, furs of the squirrel, the fox, and the beaver, feathers and other trinkets he declared belonged to the savages of Virginia. I was orphan no more. The father of the prodigal son could not have been more joyous than I, the child of the father returned from the dead.

"Why did ye leave us, Father?" I asked him when my sisters were asleep, unable to comprehend his deep grief over the loss of my mother.

"Son Giles," he answered me. "A man must provide for his family. You know I have made a fair living as a tanner here in London, but there are unknown worlds across the sea, fantastical countries where a new life can begin."

And so he told me the story of his adventures on the ship called, aptly, *Sea Venture* and what happened thereafter.

"We were seven ships: *Sea Venture, Falcon, Diamond, Swallow, Unity, Blessing,* and *Lion,* together with two vessels not as large. They be called pinnaces."

"Were ye the captain of the ship, Father?"

"By heavens, no my son. Our admiral was Sir George Summers, but our captain was Christopher Newport. And on board we had another knight, Sir Thomas Gates, appointed by the king governor of our destination: Virginia."

I sighed in amazement that Father should keep such company. "And what was your job, Father?"

"Ah, son, they had no need of a tanner on board the *Sea Venture*. Because of my knowledge of God's holy word, I was appointed clerk to our minister, Master Richard Buck. My work was to read the Scriptures--the Psalms and other chapters on Sundays.

"For Minister Buck did justify our mission to the savages in a new country from The Epistle of St. Paul to the Hebrews, to wit:

> By faith he that is called Abraham
> obeyed to go out into a place which he was
> to receive for an inheritance. And he went
> out, not knowing whither he went. . . .

By faith he abode in the land of
promise, as in a strange country, dwelling in
cottages, with Isaac and Jacob, the co-heirs
of the same promise.

For he looked for a city that hath
foundations: whose builder and maker is
God.

Did ye not have faith I would return, son?"

"I did doubt ye would, Father. I was told you were
dead after my mother died."

My father now quoted from the new translation
commissioned by our most exalted and Christian King James.
Father ever embraced that which was new under the infinite
and wise benevolence of Almighty God, unlike the Puritans,
who even now cling to the old ways and the old translation of
the Scriptures from Geneva. He said, "'Oh ye of little faith'!
Remember, child, the words of our Lord and Savior, Jesus
Christ, as He spoke on the mount:

And why take ye thought for your
raiment? Consider the lilies of the field, how
they grow; they toil not, neither do they spin:

And yet I say unto you, That even
Solomon in all his glory was not arrayed like
one of these.

Wherefore, if God so clothe the grass
of the field, which to day is, and to morrow is
cast into the oven, shall he not much more
clothe you, O ye of little faith?

Therefore take no thought, saying,
What shall we eat? or, What shall we drink?
or, Wherewithal shall we be clothed?
As it pleased God, you were not wanting in food and clothing and shelter, were ye, my son Giles?"

I had to say I was not. "Well then, though He took your dear mother, it pleased God to bring me back to father you and your sisters and to bring you to a new land as were Abraham and Joshua given the lands God intended for their inheritance."

This gave me pause for thought. Little though I was in stature and in years, from the time of my childish troubles the Lord has blessed me with keen powers of thought. "What about those Indians you have told me about, Father? Is it not their land already?"

"Ye are a right smart lad, my boy, and filled with compassion like that of our Lord." This made my heart swell.

"Yet many of those said Indians are no better than the Philistines who God gave the power to smote through his servant David. Their king, Powhatan, or his braves, did cause to be killed many of our men who strayed from the fort. And he took and slaughtered our hundreds of hogs, our chicks and hens, our stallions and mares. Our Lord Governor did order to be cut off the right hand of one of King Powhatan's most incorrigible monsters. The hand was sent to Powhatan as a solemn warning not to wreak havoc on our people again."

"And did ye see this, Father?"

"Yea, indeed I did and many other strange and amazing things. Yet I have known many good and wise and generous members of that people some say are children of the lost tribes of Israel. No harm was done to me, though I

19

mingled with them, learning their manner of planting, hunting, and fishing.

"If ye like, I will take you and your sisters to see one of these selfsame 'savages,' who, against their will were seized and brought to this country for the amusement of the king, his court, and the commoners on the streets."

"Oh yes, Father. I should very much like to see an Indian. But ye haven't told me about your terrible ship wreck in the Bermudas."

"I will tell ye, but now it is time for sleep: 'To every thing there is a season, and a time to every purpose under the heaven.'"

"Yes, Father," I said. And from their corner bed I heard my sisters moan unhappily. I could not ascertain any words.

SHORTLY HE CAME to tell us, for my sisters were listening that night, of the terrible events that led to the wrecking of the ship *Sea Venture* in the Bermudas. "Storms," he said, "are not uncommon on the turbulent seas 'twixt England and Virginia.

"A tempest came from the northeast and with hideous thunder and lightning and rain did hit our poor vessel so hard that I thought I would be like Jonah, cast into the mouth of some grotesque sea creature. Indeed, it seemed as though the ship itself would be broken in twain under a torrent hard as a thousand cannons bursting upon an enemy of war.

"After twenty-four hours of this torment, we thought the tempest to have done its worst. Prayers lifted from our lips were lost in the noise of shouts from our officers and the constant wind, and still the storm raged, gathering strength, as 'twere, from the breath of God Almighty.

"The officers did creep about the ship with candles cupped in their hands to discover where the water found an opening in the boards, for the *Sea Venture,* she had sprung a powerful leak and the water threatened to take our very breath from our bodies.

"Naked we were who were not officers as we worked four nights and three days with no sleep or food, throwing out our luggage and our stores of victuals, tossing out the water to no avail.

"On the Thursday night Sir George Summers, having taken watch duty like any other sailor, saw, and I quote the account circulated about London by my fellow passenger, William Strachey, 'an apparition of a little round light, like a faint Starre, trembling, and streaming along with a sparkeling blaze, halfe the height upon the Maine Mast, and shooting sometimes from Shroud to Shroud, tempting to settle as it were upon any of the foure Shrouds.' This lasted for hours through the night, departing and coming back. Sir George called the men to observe the phenomenon, and the sailors called it 'Sea-fire,' and I have heard it called 'Corpo sancto' by the Italians and 'Saint Elmo's Fire,' by the Spaniards. Master Buck said the Greeks in the Mediterranean Sea called such an apparition 'Castor and Pollux,' and that if only one appeared, it portended a storm of great and heinous destruction.

"The Greeks were surely right, for soon the sea rose like a great colossus twenty times the size of London Bridge and, as Strachey says, the 'confluence of water was so violent, as it rusht and carried the Helm-man from the Helme, and wrested the Whip-staffe out of his hand, which so flew from side to side, that when he would have ceased to same againe, it so tossed him from Star-boord to Lar-boord, as it was Gods mercy it had not split him.' Governor Gates exhorted us to work harder, an exhortation so unnecessary I was prepared to say we worked harder than the devil himself when a rush of water dashed me to the deck like a piece of meat the butcher slaps on his cutting board.

"Just as we were ready to surrender our wretched souls unto God and the ship to the sea, Sir George cried out, 'Land-ho! Land-ho!' It was the Bermudas, called the Devil's Islands, but no greater savior, apart from our Lord, could have presented itself at this, our most mortal hour.

"Alas, the ship foundered on two immense stones, a mile or less from the shore. Yet these Islands, hitherto avoided by sailors as inhabited by evil spirits, became both our means of salvation and our sustenance for the nine or ten months following, for they were an earthly paradise, buffeted by storms, yes, but also providing soil to grow from those of our own seeds as survived the wreck: musk melons, peas, onions, radish, lettuce and herbs. I never saw a frog or serpent, only spiders and wild hogs, too, which, though they dug into our gardens, provided delicious meat, hunted down with our ship's dog--boars, sows, and piglets alike. God was pleased to provide marvelous turtles and their eggs, large as those of our geese, as food for our meals. Also there were palms of many kinds, coco, date, and palmetto, and fish from the sea and the brooks that sailed into it, and all manner of fowl: little birds, fat sparrows, larger than those we have in England, robins of many shades of yellow and green. In addition to these there were owls and bats and many seabirds such as the giant cormorant and the swan."

It was long past our sleeping time and Elizabeth had already slipped into the land of Morpheus and Constance was well on her way. As for myself, my eyes could not have been wider.

10 FEBRUARY 1864, BOSTON

HERE THE NARRATIVE stops, only to resume at a later date, I assume, because the handwriting, though clearly that of Giles Hopkins, is altered somewhat, and the paper is different. My guess is that, although the mutiny of his father was surely known among many of the passengers on the *Mayflower* and the later inhabitants of Plymouth, Stephen Hopkins must no doubt have refrained from telling his children the awful details. Even had he related the story to Giles, I doubt his son would repeat it in his memoir.

I have consulted my brother and sister as to whether they think I am doing the right thing to transcribe the memoir of Giles and to think of publishing it. James asked me how I could take the time from my business for such a laborious task. I told him there was a lull in the business and that my assistant could handle the day-to-day activities. My work on Giles's memoir is not so strenuous that I can not supervise the business. I go in once or twice a week to keep an eye on things and attend to any problems that might arise.

And yet during the night after my talk with James, like a ghost from a story by the renowned English novelist, Charles Dickens, a figure appeared at the foot of my bed. I was as frightened as Scrooge when I realized it was Aunt Huldah hovering above the bed. She seemed to warn me: "Stop! Go no further!"

"What do you mean?" I asked. "Why?" But she disappeared as quickly as she had come. I remembered her last words, "the Apostle Paul." A chill ran through my bones. I sat up and wiped my eyes with my bare fingers. I lit a candle, and, after some quick reflection, I dismissed what had happened as a mere superstitious apparition. I went back to sleep.

THERE IS A family rumor about Stephen Hopkins's near execution, but I had never given it much thought since it occurred in an era well over two hundred years before my own. The local library answered my questions by providing the very book, *Purchas His Pilgrimes,* that published the narrative by William Strachey Stephen Hopkins boldly quotes from. Whether he knew that his adventures accounted in part for the inspiration of that farewell play by William Shakespeare called *The Tempest* I do not know. He must have heard rumor of that drama if not witnessed it himself.

Surely the Stephano portrayed by Shakespeare's *Tempest* is a figure of that great poet's imagination. Stephano is no more my ancestor than is Caliban a true representation of the native peoples of this continent.

Nevertheless, there is no getting around the fact that Stephen Hopkins committed a crime so grim it resulted in his being sentenced to hang. If there is any compensation to this horrific incident, it is that on that island mutiny thrived like Queen Anne's lace here in my native state. One of the ringmasters was in fact a Puritan thought to be of the Brownist variety. After much "sorrow and repentance," this man and his cohorts were generously pardoned by the governor. The other mutineer went so far as to strike his commanding officer repeatedly and to use language so vulgar that Mr. Strachey felt it best to leave it unrecorded. This mutineer, a Mr. Henry Paine, the governor summarily sentenced to hang. However, Paine pled his right as a gentleman to be shot and this was done, "the Sunne and his life setting together."

THE EVENTS SURROUNDING Stephen Hopkins on the Bermudas in the year 1609 I would continue to narrate in my own words, but I prefer to give my reader the quaint writing of two hundred and fifty years ago. In reference to the first mutiny, that of the Brownist and company, Mr. Strachey writes:

> Yet could not his be any warning to others, who more subtilly began to shake the foundation of our quiet safety, and therein did one Stephen Hopkins commence the first act or overture: A fellow who had much knowledge in the Scriptures, and could reason well therein, whom our Minister therefore chose to be his Clarke, to reade the Psalmes, and Chapters upon Sondayes at the Assembly of the Congregation under him: who in January the twenty foure, brake with one Samuel Sharpe and Humfrey Reede (who presently discovered it to the Governour) and alleaged substantiall arguments, both civill and divine (the Scripture falsly quoted) that it was no breach of honesty, conscience, nor Religion, to decline from the obedience of the Governour, or refuse to goe any further, led by his authority (except it so pleased themselves) since the authority ceased when the wracke was committed, and with it, they were all then freed from the government of any man; and for a matter of Conscience, it was not unknowne to the meanest, how much we were therein bound

each one to provide for himselfe, and his owne
family: for which were two apparant reasons to
stay them even in this place. . . .

And so on and so forth. The gist of his argument was that
the men and, I should say also women, for there were two
babies born, a girl named Bermuda and a boy named
Bermudas--was this the impetus for Stephen calling his own
child born on the *Mayflower* Oceanus? Also there was a
wedding, but I digress; the men, Hopkins said, had the right
to look after their own business and build their own vessels
to take them to Virginia, which in fact they eventually did.
Perhaps he quoted the scripture, here rendered in the
Authorized Version of St. Matthew 6: 24: "No man can serve
two masters."

Whatever arguments he advanced, Stephen Hopkins
was, as Strachey reports, "brought forth in manacles, and
both accused, and suffered to make at large, to every
particular, his answere; which was onely full of sorrow and
teares, pleading simplicity, and deniall." Nevertheless, he was
sentenced to death for, as the historian says, "Mutinie and
Rebellion." Mr. Strachey continues:

But so penitent hee was, and made so much
moane, alleadging the ruine of his Wife and
Children in this his trespasse, as it wrought in
the hearts of all the better sort of the Company,
who therefore with humble intreaties, and
earnest supplications, went unto our Governor,
whom they besought (as likewise did Captaine
Newport, and my selfe) and never left him untill
we had got his pardon.

I can not help but wonder whether Shakespeare had Hopkins
in mind when, during the storm of his play, *The Tempest,* some

woe begotten soul cries out: "'Farewell my wife and children!'" Such speculation, however, is idle, for we shall never know.

I continue now with the 1677 narrative of Giles Hopkins:

1617, LONDON, FROM THE MEMOIR OF GILES HOPKINS

SHORTLY AFTER FATHER told us the tale of his adventures in the Bermudas, my sister Elizabeth fell sick of the ague. Although Father applied to her fevered body leaves of the sassafras tree which he had brought with him from Virginia, my sister departed from this world and was buried with her mother at Hursley, Hampshire.

Because we mourned our Elizabeth, named after our late queen, many weeks passed before Father kept his promise to take us to see one of the savages from across the ocean. My friend, Trevor Baker, came with us. I remember two men with brown skin displayed like monkeys on a rostrum, bound together with a tether. They each had a feather on his head, secured by a band. Their long black hair was parted in the middle and hung down in braids wrapped in ribbons on their shoulders. Their faces were painted with black stripes and their arms had copper or brass bands. For garments they wore only leathern skirts. Of leather too were their leggings, which reached above their knees. The crowd so gathered around these men we could not get closer than ten or eleven yards. Regarded like animals from Africa by most of the crowd, these savages so fascinated me I have ever afterwards retained a wary affection for them. They inhabited my dreams, half savage and half civilized brown-coloured Englishmen. I saw them in their home country with bows and arrows hunting deer, foxes, boars, and other animals familiar to me.

When in 1621 we were established in our new house at Plymouth, Father entertained for a night one of these Indians, Samoset, who had come to our plantation. Because of Father, he left a friend. Samoset slept in our house, and soon in our village another Indian, Tisquantum, or Squanto as he was generally called, came. He had been in London, but he was not one of those I saw on that fateful day.

There was, however, another Indian Father had known in Jamestown. The daughter of the great chief, Powhatan, Pocahontas had married John Rolfe, whom Father also knew from Virginia. Child that I was, I knew that a thing of tremendous import was happening in London when John Rolfe and his bride Pocahontas arrived in the country and were presented at the court of our most sovereign King James. She, a princess, would never have been exhibited like those other Indians Father took Constance, Trevor, and me to see. She was a Christian, and Father said she showed that the mission to convert the Indians could be so successful Christian men could wed with formerly savage women. Were he yet in Virginia, and knowing that his beloved wife Mary had gone to Heaven, he himself might have married an Indian maiden could he find one as comely and high born as Pocahontas. It was with sincere sorrow, then, that we learned of her untimely death in 1617 while still in England, far from her native land. Father had by then begun courting Elizabeth Fisher, who, though a kindly woman, could never replace my sweet mother Mary.

1618, London, from the Memoir of Giles Hopkins

FATHER AND ELIZABETH Fisher were wed in February 1618, and later that same year my half-sister, Damaris, was born. Father said Damaris meant "wife" in Greek, and she was named in honor of his late wife, Mary, and his new wife, Elizabeth. He said it was good to have a baby girl in the house after our loss of Elizabeth. Many years later he would name his last child after his second wife and my first sister.

Many times he repeated or alluded to the story of his travels in America, and when he broached the idea of taking the entire family there, my heart leapt. "Will there be Indians, Father?" I asked.

"Not only will there be Indians but sundry other people and adventures there besides."

He never asked if we wanted to go. There was no need. My sister and stepmother's opinions were of little concern, and I was so delighted at the idea he never had to inquire my views on the subject.

I told my friend Trevor, and he too became agitated with excitement. "I want to go with ye!" he said.

"Why can ye not? Tell your father what opportunities await there."

"But my father is happy with his occupation," Trevor sighed. His father was, like his name, a baker, and made the best bread in our part of London. His father's father had been a baker as had *his* father and as far back as anyone could remember the family had followed in the footsteps of the fathers. Trevor was going to be a baker too. "They need bread in America," I said. But Trevor doubted his father would sell his shop and move to a strange new world.

So be it, I thought. My mind was filled with visions of sailing on the ocean and living in a brave new place. What that place must resemble I knew only from my father's tales, which were not all pretty. But I was a child and I thought like a child.

DIVERS MEN CAME to our house and had conversations about going to America with a group of Puritans who had separated from the King's church and moved to the Netherlands. Later I knew the names of these men. The Puritans were John Carver and William Bradford (both became governors of the new colony), and their agents were Robert Cushman and Edward Southworth. My father was a strong believer in the Church of England, yet because he had experience in the New World, and particularly with the savages who lived there, these men enticed him to go. Father's business as a leather maker prospered, but he knew, he told us, he could become a planter in America and leave land to his children. Here in England his chances for advancement were not so apparent. After his experience at sea, he said, he had come to believe any man's religion--so long as it was not Papist--was his own affair. He himself would never become a Puritan ("They are so ominously serious," he would say), but he did not see why we could not tolerate living with them.

"After the contract is complete," he told us, "we can do as we like." I did not know the contract with the "adventurers" who provided the money for the project would not expire for seven years. I did know Father would always be with us. Never again would he journey away as he did when I was a little boy. On this he gave his solemn word.

Thus it came to pass that we, the Hopkins family, became passengers on a ship called the *Mayflower* in 1620. I was nearly thirteen years of age, and I had no conception of the hardships that awaited us. As far as I could tell, no one in my family did, not even Father.

We said good-bye to my father's brother, my Uncle Caleb, who had provided nails for the settling of the new colony, and I said good-bye to Trevor, suspecting, but not really believing, we would not see each other again. "I'm going to be a sailor," I said, "and come visit ye in England."

"Right!" said Trevor as we shook hands. That did not seem sufficient, so I put my arms around him and he put his around me. Then we said our goodbyes.

1620, THE *MAYFLOWER*, FROM THE MEMOIR OF GILES HOPKINS

FATHER SOLD HIS shop, where we lived in the back of the building, and hired two servants, as I have written. They would work for him for several years until they could pay him back for the cost of their servitude.

We met the other passengers in Southampton at the end of July. We were to sail in two ships, the *Speedwell* and the much larger *Mayflower,* on which our passage was assigned. Father remarked with satisfaction that only about a third of the passengers were actually of the Separatist religion.

We set sail on 5 August. Then the troubles began. The master of the *Speedwell* sent word that his vessel was leaking. It must be repaired. To this end we sailed back to Dartmouth. When we again set sail, the *Speedwell* again leaked. Superstitiously, my father offered the opinion that the ship's name had put a spell on it. "Would that it had a more propitious appellation," he said to us in private. "At this rate we will not reach our destination till Christmas." His words became prophetic, yet we would not celebrate the holiday, for the Puritans would have none of that.

After returning to Plymouth and deciding the *Speedwell* was unseaworthy for the voyage across the Atlantic, our ship was forced to accept more passengers. We were one hundred and two altogether. We, most of us, crowded under the deck like cattle. Were it not for my making a friend of John Cooke, who was of mine own age, I would have been a lonely young lad, particularly as through all the delays I had begun to feel the absence of my home and my friend, Trevor. All my excitement had turned into gruel, tasteless as the hardtack we had to eat on board the ship.

We children had to sleep on the floor, where all manner of crawling things vexed us, and rats the ship's cat hadn't caught skittered by. We drank beer like the adults because the water in the barrels had gone rancid. The only books to read were religious, so we read the psalms and sang the songs the Separatists sang. I had a game of Nine Men's Morris, and when the water was calm John and I would play with other boys and girls.

My father was not too pleased with my friendship with John, for his father, Francis, was a Separatist, and Father mistrusted the Separatists more than he would say. Yet he was none too pleased with some of the non-Separatists. Francis Billington, for one, nearly blew all of us into pieces when he burnt a rope by the gunpowder barrels. His face turned so red I laughed when Father's head was turned. After that Father told me to be careful not to get into any mischief with Francis Billington. While anchored at Cape Cod Francis again created trouble by shooting a fowling piece. Father offered his opinion that the Puritans must have been crazy to bring along such malcontents as the Billingtons.

Then the storms came and another young person, man servant to John Carver, fell into the sea when the ship tipped. God was good to John Howland, for he caught a long rope from the topsail and the sailors brought him in.

By this time the sea was tossing us as if we were helpless kittens--just as in the stories my father had told so many times. My stomach was at my throat and all my hardtack and salted meat and fish was at my feet or in the face of whoever was near me. Alas for John, he no sooner had lost his dinner on the deck than he got mine smack in his face! It was the tossing of the ship that did it. This was not the adventure I anticipated it would be. I lay ill for days on days while the ship tossed and turned and water leaked into our quarters till we were soaked to the skin. I had never been so sick.

My stepmother was with child, and I feared, as did my father and sister, she would lose the baby and herself. But she was a hardy woman and determined. As the Puritans said, the Lord was with her: she delivered a baby boy called, after the sea, Oceanus. His mother's cries were drowned by the howling of the wind and rain, yet not she, nor anyone else, was drowned.

We lost only two to the fate that awaits all mortals: William Butten, servant to our doctor, Samuel Fuller, and the odious sailor who tormented those of us in the orlop beneath his feet. Will got sick with a fever and perished. And the muscular young sailor, who with nasty cursing upbraided the Separatists, saying he was happy they were sick and wished he could throw half of them into the sea, this young man was

himself struck sick unto death, and his fellow sailors slipped
him overboard before our voyage was over.

AFTER OUR LANDING at Cape Cod in November
1620, my father gave me great pride, for, though he was not a
Separatist, he was called upon by the Puritan leaders to assist
them in their explorations and dealings with the native
inhabitants of the land many times. In various accounts I
have read and heard about they do give him credit, yet no one
has recorded his opinions on these matters.

After my father died at age 62 in 1644, I found among
his papers copies of letters he wrote to his brother, my uncle,
Caleb. I insert them here to help complete my narrative.

18 NOVEMBER 1620, THE *MAYFLOWER*, LETTER OF STEPHEN HOPKINS TO HIS BROTHER, CALEB

TO MY HIGHLY valued and loved brother, Caleb:

Knowing ye have some interest in our adventure here
and in the welfare of your only brother and his family, I write
to tell ye by the grace of God we have arrived safely in the
New World. We are at Cape Cod, not, as we proposed and as
our patent called for, in Northern Virginia at the Hudson
River. Having been delayed in England due to insupportable
trouble--leakings and the like--with the ship *Speedwell*, we have
arrived here at the onset of winter. Shallow water and bad
weather prevented our sailing to the Hudson River, so as our
stubborn-minded leaders have decided, we are here in what I
dare say is a colder, more harsh country.

Be that as it may, certain of our leaders, Wm.
[William] Bradford, Ed[ward] Winslow, &c, found it pertinent
to draw up an agreement as to the governing of the colony,
this due to divers murmurings of mutiny to the effect that

since we have not and will not settle in the territory of our patent, when we dis-embarque we shall be free agents to do as we will. You will recognize in this argument similarities to my own statements on the Bermudas (or Somer Ilands as they are called) which led to the unfortunate consequence against me there. In spite of their knowledge of my actions there, said persons above requested my presence in this venture, and I assure ye I was not among those who muttered mutinous ideas. I am not a foolish man.

Be that as it may, those in control of the enterprise wrote down an agreement to prevent any such mutinies from occurrence, and asked those of us who might, may I say it, perpetuate said mutinies, together with the men of the Separatist company, to sign it. This we did. You may find the document rather curious coming from those who suffered great persecution from the sovereign King James so that they departed from the countrie to Holland. In spite of that, and perchance due to the reason of their lack of a legal patent, they made us sign this, a copy of which Mr. Bradford provided me for reasons I reckon ye may understand:

We whose names are underwritten, the loyal subjects of our dread Sovereign Lord King James, by the Grace of God of Great Britain, France, and Ireland King, Defender of the Faith, etc.

Having undertaken, for the Glory of God and advancement of the Christian Faith and Honour of our King and Country, a Voyage to plant the First Colony in the Northern Parts of Virginia, do by these presents solemnly and mutually in the presence of God and one of another, Covenant and Combine ourselves

together into a Civil Body Politic, for our better
ordering and preservation and furtherance of
the ends aforesaid; and by virtue hereof to
enact, constitute and frame such just and equal
Laws, Ordinances, Acts, Constitutions and
Offices, from time to time, as shall be thought
most meet and convenient for the general good
of the Colony, unto which we promise all due
submission and obedience. In witness whereof
we have hereunder subscribed our names at
Cape Cod, the 11th of November, in the year of
the reign of our Sovereign Lord King James, of
England, France and Ireland the eighteenth, and
of Scotland the fifty-fourth. Anno Domini
1620.

Mr. John Carver was selected as the first governor of our
colony, and thereafter murmurs of mutiny ceased. I could
not help but sense the eyes of those who previously
complained looking toward me, as if they expected a mutual
support which I was unwilling to give, having with me my
wife and children to preserve and protect.

Among my family, I should tell ye, is a new member,
one Oceanus, born whilst we were at sea. Elizabeth, I fear,
suffered greatly, being with child and having to give birth
among strangers as tempests caused great havoc and
seasickness on the ship. But she is of most hardy English
stock and is possessed of a gentle disposition, as ye know,
having known her in Old England, as I may call it, writing, as
I am, from New England.

HERE THE LETTER stops; it resumes a bit later as my father's
adventures proceeded:

Our shallop, having been damaged during the many tempests that beset us at sea and by those who slept in her, we unshipped and put her on shore so that our carpenter might repair her. All of us being filthy from 66 days at sea, our apparel especially needed cleansing, we had our women wash them as all passengers likewise cleaned their bodies.

The shallop, said our carpenter, would not be ready for five or six days or more. Sundry of us able-bodied men offered to explore the territory to look for what it might contain. I was among the first chosen to do this with Captain Miles Standish, Wm Bradford, and Edward Tilley, together with twelve others, each with our muskets, swords, and armor.

After tramping one behind the other for about one English mile, we beheld five or six savages with a dog. I knew them to be Indians at once, for as ye are aware I knew them in Virginia, yet others of our party first deemed them to be Master Jones and some of his sailors, for they also had left the ship.

Captain Standish, in honor of my experience among the savages, called me to him, and we tracked them for nine or ten miles till it became dark and we were forced to set camp. Some went to fetch wood for a fire, whilst others set up a kind of barricade. We agreed to stand sentinel by turns through the night.

The following day we proceeded. For provisions, we had only hardtack, cheese from Holland, and one small bottle of aquavitae. The countrie was thick with bare trees and bushes, and we tore our corslets as we stumbled down hills and brushed against the plants till, terribly thirsty, we discovered a spring of clear water and drank as if we had never drunk before, our first drink of such delicious water in Cape Cod.

The country reminded me of Virginia, except it was bitter cold, more cold than ever I knew in England or anywhere else. It cut my face like a dozen bee bites. There were goodly vines, many wild ducks and geese, deer, and sassafras trees. Also, we found fewer Indians than I had encountered in Virginia. They seemed afeared to show their faces. Yet in many places we found signs of their habitation. We saw places where corn had been cultivated, an abundance of walnut trees filled with walnuts. We saw supplies of dried strawberries. We found mounds of sand, one of them with reed or bark mats atop, also a mortar made of wood and a clay pot. Digging beneath these things, we found a bow and some rotted arrows. I said these must be graves, and Mr. Bradford and others agreed we should let them alone. It would be hateful to "ransack their sepulchres," as he said.

At length we came upon the ruins of an Indian dwelling, with only some olden planks, about five of them connected to each other. Together with these we found evidence of others of our kind, for there lay a kettle from a ship that came from Europe. Nearby was a fresh mound of sand, and in it we discovered a small basket filled with fresh corn. Digging further, we found a newly fashioned basket with near 40 spikes of corn. The others expressed amazement at the colors of the kernels, for they were yellow, red, and blue, but I was not amazed, having witnessed such before.

Now I must tell you that I did not approve of what next they did, which was to pilfer as much of the spikes as they could stuff into the kettle, together with as many of the separate kernels as would fit and some beans to boot, so much that two were needed to carry the kettle. The rest of us were too laden with our armor. Mr. Bradford promised to recompense the natives when we could, but I wondered how he could ever find the particular people whose store they were stealing, and I wondered what they, who professed to believe our Lord's words, to wit, "And as ye would that men should do to you, do ye also to them likewise," what would they do had the savages so stolen from them. I kept my peace as one whose motives were already suspect. Yet I counted this as one of many contradictions in their professions of faith, for Mr. Bradford thanked providence for providing provision for us rather than thanking the Indians.

We found what appeared to be the ruins of a fort made by others from Europe. Yet as we had promised to be away but two days, and darkness was coming on, we had hastily to create a barricado for the night, which was very wet from the rain, which still did not prevent our lighting a large fire for the satisfaction of those on board the ship.

My singular worth to the company was proven, I believe, beyond dispute the next morning when we dallied about before a boat from the ship came to take us back. For I espied a trap for a deer made by the natives of the countrie--a sapling bent over a bow with acorns spread under it and a strong hemp rope with a noose to catch the deer. I knew this device from others I had seen in Virginia. Without delay I warned the men of its danger, but Wm Bradford, apparently having not heard--or listened?--stepped into the thing, which directly caught his leg and turned him upside down as 'twere. The absurdity of the sight caused me to laugh, but I turned face about to stifle my amusement whilst I heard others who also laughed. I assisted some of the men in getting Mr. Bradford out of the trap he had so adroitly fallen into.

When we had fired our pieces and the boat came to convey us back, we were greeted by many exclamations of joy, especially that we were safe and had found corn seed to be planted for harvest. Dear brother, I admit I was glad to take credit for some of our success, notwithstanding my opinions about the manner in which we obtained the corn and beans.

From the *Mayflower*, Cape Cod, 18th of November, 1620.

Your loving and loyal brother,
Stephen Hopkins

Here the first part of the manuscript by Giles Hopkins ends with his signature.

Chapter Two
Stephen Hopkins, emissary to the Indians, together with the early History of Plymouth Colony, Massasoit and his brother, Quadequina, etc.

2 March 1864, Eastham, Cape Cod

I HAVE DECIDED for the time being to work on my transcription here in Eastham at the home of my aunt. Her late husband prospered as a seaman, and he built a comfortable two-story brick house which always served well for family gatherings. At the time the house was built they had two children, but tragically, each one died--one from a drowning accident, one from diphtheria--and after the second birth the doctor said Huldah must not attempt another birth. My brother, sister, and I were the beneficiaries of my aunt and uncle's misfortunes, for they spoiled us as children, giving us more than my father, a librarian in Salem, could ever afford.

It is just as cold here as it is in Boston this time of year, but within a month or two spring will be here and it will be lovely living on Cape Cod, so near the ocean, for a change. Soon, of course, I shall have to sell the house and give my brother and sister their parts of the inheritance, but they are in no hurry, I am pleased to say. Periodically I will have to return to Boston to attend to my business, but for now I may relax and transcribe these papers at my leisure.

I hesitate to add, both because I fear it is mere superstition mixed with grief on my part and because it may lower the price of the house, that the ghostly appearances of

Aunt Huldah have become more frequent now that I am living at her house. Now she utters her last words with increasingly annoying and frightening repetition: "Leviticus . . . the Apostle Paul." I am still at a loss as to what specifically she refers. I loved my aunt, but I must confess she was foolishly attached to her religion.

The reader may well question the truth of the documents so far transcribed. When I have finished my transcription of the remaining papers, and after I have published them, I will gladly make them available to the public at an appropriate place,-- a museum of American history perhaps, or, more likely, an esteemed university such as Harvard, let us say, or Brown.

Giles Hopkins continues his journal with another letter from his father to his uncle, Caleb Hopkins.

28 DECEMBER 1620, NEW PLYMOUTH, LETTER OF STEPHEN HOPKINS TO HIS BROTHER, CALEB

MOST ESTEEMED BROTHER,

I write again, knowing not when or indeed whether ye shall receive these letters. You must not forget the difficulties of the season. The season was not propitious for exploration, never mind setting our feet down in a new colony. Freezing snow and rain threatened to fall at any moment and did.

After two more days our shallop was ready and we set out thirty-four of us. This time Master Jones was our leader. No sooner had we set out in the long boat and shallop than it began to snow and the wind chilled as if to freeze us all. The water was too shallow for the shallop to come to shore, so several of us men set up a barricado, a fire, and sentinels for the night. Late the next morning the shallop joined us at the river we had before discovered and named Cold Harbor. It was not a harbor for ships, only for smaller boats and such when the water was high. We marched some miles, shooting four plump geese and seven ducks which we, being famished, devoured like animals.

We marched to the place where before we had taken the corn with the many-colored ears and confiscated some more. Mr. Winslow estimated our total now was close to ten bushels, plenty for seed to feed the colony next year. Not yet a planter myself I took him at his word, doubting, as I have indicated, what the consequences would be when the Indians would discover what we had done.

Again the weather began to howl and Master Jones desired to return to the ship. Mr. Winslow and Mr. Carver, being our *de facto* leaders, sent him back, together with the most weak of our company and all the corn, leaving about 18 of us to stay the night. Master Jones was to return on the morrow with our spades and mattocks to aid our explorations.

The next day, seeing a path they thought would lead to wigwams, I told them it was only a hunting path to catch deer. The Indians have many paths through the woods, very narrow and very efficient to their purposes, yet not easy for Europeans to detect. Soon we came upon a large grave and, though I cautioned against it, the leaders and other men were fain to discover what it contained, forgetting Mr. Bradford's admonition against ransacking their graves. They found a mat, beneath which was a fine bow together with various kitchen items (plates, bowls and the like), then another mat and more such "trinkets," as Mr. Winslow called them, and then a delicately shaped and painted board with three well-carved prongs atop. Under a third mat we found finely ground red ochre atop the skeleton of a man. Still on the skull was a thin yellow growth of hair and skin. It was a European corpse, for it was wrapped in a seaman's canvas garment and a sailor's breeches. Also wrapped among the bones were a packneedle, a knife, and some things made of iron.

Upon further examination, we discovered the bones of a small child wrapt with lines and bracelets covered with pretty white beads. Again the men pilfered the goods, taking what they liked best. Dear brother, again I must confess my own shortcoming, for I too took a bracelet, thinking to give it to Elizabeth as a token of my love for her and our new baby.

Then ensued a debate as to the identity of the man with the yellow hair. Some believed the Indians were white men like us, perhaps the lost tribes of Israel, for they lived in tribes and had divers other habits conforming to those we read of in the Bible. This must be proof of such. Others said no Jew or Indian he knew of had yellow hair. They all of them had black hair. Perchance this was a special person, a king among the savages. Others said it must be a sailor from Europe because of his clothing. Still others said he was a sacrifice to the gods of the savages and thus buried with honor. As for me, I knew, as did the others, Europeans had penetrated these parts. In point of fact, there are rumors that the Norsemen--the Vikings that had ransacked our countrie and the world--had sailed to the New World to do the same. Yet this man was newly buried, with skin still intact. He could not be a Viking, but he could be a Frenchman, an Englishman, or even a Dutchman. How then to account for the child buried with him?

Our debate never came to a satisfactory conclusion, particularly as two of our company found two Indian dwellings recently fled from. They were made round from saplings bent with each end fixed in the ground. The saplings were securely covered with tightly wrought, strong mats, both inside and out, and with a hole in the middle above for smoke. This and the door, three feet high, had mats to cover them. A man could stand fully erect inside. Stakes were driven into the ground with sticks placed upon them for pots to hang. The household must have slept on the mats that lay around the fire. We saw kitchen ware, clay pots, sundry baskets woven and made of crab shells and the like together with an English bucket. Also there were the heads of deer, one of them fresh, a clutter of deer's feet hanging in the wigwams, horns of harts, and claws of eagles and, what was as remarkable, baskets of dried acorns, slices of fish, and a cutting of herring, already cooked. We saw also some silken grass, tobacco seed, and other unknown seeds. Outside was various stuff for the making of mats: long leaves, sedge, and rushes, etc. Venison was stuck in some of the trees, but it was so spoiled we gave it to the dogs. Again we pilfered the best goods, even though the people plainly left in a hurry and might well return. It was regretted that we had forgot to bring beads or other trinkets to truck with them, but when the time came we would "give them full satisfaction," as Mr. Winslow stated. Again I held my peace.

Here there is a brief gap in the letter. It resumes thus:

We undertook one more expedition of discovery before we settled at the place we are now--New Plymouth, so named on the map by Cap. John Smith and so called by us after the port we finally set sail from in England. These men, beside myself, took part: Captain Myles Standish, Gov. John Carver, Wm. [William] Bradford, Ed[ward] Winslow,

John Tilley, Ed[ward] Tilley, John Howland, he who was nearly lost at sea, Richard Warren, my servant Edward Dotey (Warren, Dotey, and myself all coming from London), John Allerton, Tho[mas] English, Master Mate Clarke, Master Gunner Coppin, and three of their sailors.

We set out on the shallop on a clear day that hours later turned to ugly weather. Water that fell on our clothes froze so hard it was like wearing double iron corslets. At length we found a place good enough to land. Down the shore we saw perhaps a dozen Indians working on a large black object. The next day we discovered it was a kind of grampus, a sort of small whale, several of which we saw dead on the shore or in the water. The Indians had begun to cut it up before they espied our party. These, together with the larger whales we saw in the deeper water, we thought would provide plenty of oil if we could harvest them.

We came upon more graves, without, I am glad to say, molesting them as we did before. Also we found corn from last year, baskets of dried acorns, and several abandoned dwellings such as we had before seen but with no mats to cover the saplings. We continued our explorations until dusk, when we set up our barricade and fire for the night.

Just about midnight we heard a loud and fearful cry as from a pack of wolves. One of the sailors declared he had often heard such cries in Newfoundland. After prayers and breakfast in the morning, we began to prepare to return to the ship on the shallop when one of our men came running and yelling, "They are here. Indians! Indians!" And arrows came flying at us. We hastened to find our muskets while Captain Standish and another of our company fired shots with their muskets. Cap. Standish told us to wait to take aim before shooting.

The cries of the Indians were fearful, just like the cry of the night before. Some of them fled, but one lively and courageous young warrior used a tree for protection and shot three arrows at us. Our men fired three musket shots at him before he turned and, with a dreadful cry, ran away unhurt with the others of the savages. Leaving some men to watch our shallop, we pursued them into the woods, shouting our weaker English shouts as we went. We did this lest they think we were afeared of them.

No man was touched by an arrow, yet those of our clothes we had hung to dry were shredded by them. "Thanks be to God! He has delivered us from our enemies," said Wm. Bradford and and the others answered, "Hear, hear! and Amen!" They called this place "First Encounter." And so, my brother, now ye know my part in its history.
From New Plimoth, 28 December, 1620.

Your loving and devoted brother,
Stephen Hopkins

My father, Stephen Hopkins (so Giles continues), was chosen to assist in many other ways in the Separatists' relations with the Indians, and I will recall come of these incidents.

1620-1621, THE *MAYFLOWER* AND NEW PLYMOUTH, FROM THE MEMOIR OF GILES HOPKINS

FIRST I WISH to write more about my own experience. Most of the women and children had to live on the ship till houses could be erected for us in the new colony. Mother, as I now called my father's wife, was so busy with the care of Oceanus, my new brother, and my little sister, Damaris, that, even with the help of my older sister and me, she had little time to fret about the discomforts we suffered from, having to sleep within inches of people we knew not before the voyage and who had become so oppressive with their complaints and illnesses. The *Mayflower*, which had carried wine and other cargo from England to France, Norway, Germany, etc., had long lost its sweet wine smell to the stink of humanity packed together like salted fish in a barrel.

While Father was out on the last exploration during which the men decided to settle at Plymouth, many of the women and the older girls began to complain that they wished they had never come here, that the bitter cold, the barren sand and leafless trees were a hell on earth compared to the lush, green country in England and in Holland with their predictable cities and orderly farms.

One late evening as I stole unto the upper deck to empty our chamber pot and to free myself from the stinking, thick air where we dwelt, I observed a grown woman fall over the side of the ship as if someone had slightly pushed her. But she was alone. I dropped the pot and ran to the fo'c'sle, where the sailors slept. We could see nothing in the dark water below. "Ah, ye was only adreamin'," said a seaman. "There weren't no lady jumpin' overboard."

I began to imagine he was right 'till next morning when the sailors discovered her body. It was Dorothy Bradford, wife of William. None dare say she took her own life. Master Bradford said it was an "accident," and if he grieved he grieved alone. No tears came from his eyes, and when the service for Mistress Bradford was held he did quote from The Gospel of St. Matthew 16: 24-25:

> Jesus then said to his disciples, If any
> man will follow me let him forsake himselfe,
> and take up his crosse, and follow me.

48

For whosoever will save his life, shall
lose it: and whosoever shall lose his life for
my sake, shall find it.

And he said: "For the sake of a new kingdom of God in this
New World, a shining city on a hill, my beloved wife Dorothy
has lost her life. As she commended her soul to Christ our
Lord, so I commend her soul to Him."

CHRISTMAS CAME AFTER our ship had removed to
Plymouth, and my family and some of the others wished to
celebrate in such little ways as we could, and especially after
so long in the wilderness of uncertainty as it were. Father
was away chopping trees to build the common house. We
had our chest with our household belongings in it, and
Mother brought out a bit of oatmeal that had survived the
voyage. She made that into a little cake and had my sister
Constance to ask the cook in the fo'c'sle to bake it for us.
Some of the other non-Separatist families did the same. The
Billingtons were among them, but not my new friend John
Cooke, for he and his father did not believe in Christmas.
We lit candles and sang some Christmas songs when,
of a sudden, William Bradford barged in upon us. "What is
this?" he said. "We'll have no festivities today. It is against
my conscience and those of us who were persecuted in
England and had thus to flee to a foreign country to find
freedom to practice our faith. This day is a Popish holiday
made from a pagan Roman holiday. It is no more holy than
every other day. Ye must stop your singing forthwith and
carry on as before." I don't know what Father would have
done were he there. When he came back and heard what had

taken place, he got us beers to drink and we said a quiet Christmas prayer.

Next year nobody dared celebrate Christmas except a few newcomers whom Gov. Bradford similarly upbraided when they left off work on Christmas day and began to play stool-ball, bar pitching, and other similar sports. After that we were cowed into keeping Christmas to ourselves at home. We no more celebrated Easter either, nor All Saint's Day, St. Valentine's Day, nor any of the holy days we had been used to honor.

DURING THE HOURS on board the *Mayflower* when I was done playing with John and my other new friends and I lay on the blankets that served for my bed, my memory drifted back to London and my friend Trevor. Although I entertained the idea of becoming a sailor and sailing to England to see him again, a voice inside me insisted that would never happen. Thoughts of my mother and my older sister visited me as well, loved ones I knew I would never see again this side of Heaven. I am not ashamed to say that more than once I fell to sleep with tears in my eyes.

Our house in Plymouth was not at all like our sturdy house in England with its fine windows and wood floors. No, our Plymouth house did not match the picture I had in my head of our New World dwelling. We had no outhouse or privy, only the wild woods and the chamber pot. Made of wattle and daub, outer walls constructed of clapboards such as the colony would make and send to England in partial satisfaction of our debt to the adventurers, its roof was thatched with reeds, the earthen floor covered with rushes.

Each family on the *Mayflower* had brought something to provide protection against witches. Father, whether he believed in witches or not, wanted to give the Separatist authorities no excuse to frown upon his behavior, and, I believe, he wanted protection from witches in case we needed it. So from our chest he procured and buried in the foundation of our house an ox bone he had got from the butcher in London. We could not lay a brick glazed with salt in the chimney to ward off witches coming in that way because we had no bricks. However, Father had bought a pretty German witch bottle, called a Bartmann, furnished with the face of a satyr and rounded body like a bowl. This he polished with salt and buried beneath what served as a hearth for the corner fire. Lastly, just above our door, Father placed a horseshoe made of iron.

Thus well protected against any witches, devils, or other evil spirits, our first house stood next to that of John Howland on the corner of an intersection across from the house of William Bradford, soon to be governor after the sudden death of John Carver. We were more fortunate that some others because, though we had but one room, we had a chimney, not a mere hole above to let the smoke out. My parents had their bed with green curtains, and we had a long wooden table on which much work and eating was done.

Across from Master Bradford's house was the house of the Billingtons, and by them were the Cookes, Francis and John. John's mother, Hester, a Walloon Separatist born in Canterbury, did not arrive till 1623 on the *Anne*, together with John's sister, Jane, and his brother, Jacob. When John told me how fortunate I was to have all my family with me, I told him how I missed my Mother and sister Elizabeth and my friend, Trevor. "Ah, you are right," John would say. "At least I have hope of seeing my mother and my sister and brother again in this world."

ONE BY ONE we left the *Mayflower* as dwellings were built for us. Boys like John and me were told to mix daub or gather wood for fires, when we were well, that is. Sad to say, one by one members of our company grew sick and died. Many times I felt as if I myself might die and almost wished it as a welcome release from the chills I felt, the fevers, and the aches in my body.

Our family, praise be to God, was spared, as were my friend, John, and his father. The Billingtons likewise were spared, but by spring half the company had perished, both those who called themselves the "Saints" and we they called the "Strangers." I need not add that by then certainly we were no strangers to each other as we had all shared in the sufferings and deprivations of what Masters Bradford and Brewster and others were pleased to call the "Promised Land."

Francis Billington and his brother John sometimes joined with me and John Cooke to play a game of marbles whilst on board the ship. Francis was not always getting into trouble, as my earlier remarks might suggest. Both he and his brother were restless boys, and one day not long after we had come to Plymouth, he climbed a tall tree and espied what it seemed to him was a large sea. Later he took one of the ship mates to see it. They walked about three miles and found a great body of water, two large lakes as it were, which are called the Billington Sea.

Yet it seemed the Billingtons were never far from troubling the colony and themselves. In June of our first year John, the younger, drifted off by himself until he got lost in the country of the Nausets where Father and the others had explored the last winter. Ten of our men, with my father, together with Squanto and another Indian friend,

Tokamahamon, set out by shallop to recover him. A storm arose, and the party stopped at Barnstable, then called Cummaquid.

The next morning, Father told me, they did see savages collecting lobsters. The party sent Squanto and Tokamahamon to ask about the boy. The savages said he was fine but not there. He was at Nauset (today called Eastham, where I presently reside). The Indians invited the party to come ashore and they fed them, afterwards bringing them to their sachem, Iyanough, a young man of about twenty-six, a well-mannered, friendly, and comely person, very unlike a savage save for his apparel.

I well remember the terrible story Father heard there from an old woman who looked to be a hundred years of age. Never before had she seen men from England, yet she had a most bitter and tearful tale to tell. Her three sons had been captured by Captain Thomas Hunt about seven years before, leaving her without the care and love of her sons in her elderly years. Squanto said he knew these men, who had been sold as slaves in Spain. He himself was one of the twenty-four or so captured Indians, but his good fortune was to have escaped and gone to England, where he learned English and later returned to his own land, Patuxet, where Plymouth now lay. There he found none of his people, for all but a few who ran away had fallen victim to the plague. Having learnt English, he now served as chief interpreter for Plymouth.

Father said that Mr. Winslow, he, and the others were very grieved by the old woman's story and told her that the Englishman who had taken her sons was evil and ought to be punished for what he did. The party all assured her they would never do such a thing. But of course other Englishmen, if they did not kill them, sold into slavery in the

Indies vanquished Pequot warriors about sixteen years later, and Englishmen did the same after the recent conflict called King Philip's War to the wife and son of King Philip and many others. This was all to come, however. These Englishmen gave the woman some beads and a scarf or two and left her a little comforted.

Iyanough provided the men their dinner, and they set sail for Nauset, sending Squanto on ahead to explain to Aspinet, the Nauset sachem, the nature of their errand. Upon landing, the men were, as Father said, apprehensive, for these were the Indians who had shot arrows at them at the beach they call First Encounter. The company held up their muskets as a hoard of Indians surrounded them. Using Squanto as their interpreter, they bid two of them to come forward. One of these was an owner of the corn the men had taken during their explorations the past winter. The man was promised he would be recompensed for his corn if he would come to Patuxet, or they said they could bring the corn to him. He said he would come to the village.

While there, the men attempted to trade for some fur. They were able to obtain just a little.

At dusk, Aspinet marched to the shallop with great ceremony and over a hundred men, half unarmed and half with bows and arrows. He handed over the boy, John Billington, who had several wampum strings around his neck and, Father said, wore a stupid grin. The men made peace with Aspinet, giving him a knife and another knife to the man who first found the boy in the woods, surviving on berries growing there.

AS THE ABLE-BODIED men and we boys, such as we could, helped construct the common house and other family

54

houses, others as I have said were sick unto death, particularly in the biting cold months of January and February. In addition to my brother, Oceanus, another baby, Peregrine White, was born on the *Mayflower*, whilst we were anchored at Cape Cod. Rather than his mother, Susanna, dying in the general sickness that plagued us, and as you might expect in her weakened condition (and as too often happened to women who bore children), Peregrine's father, William, expired on 21 February. All the More children, aristocratic bastards one and all, were apportioned to different families, and all died but Richard, who was attached as ward to Elder William Brewster (ah, so many Williams we had on the *Mayflower*!). Master Winslow's wife died on 24 March. Whole families died, such as Tom Tinker, his wife and son. Couples such as John and Alice Rigdale and James and Mrs. Chilton perished, as did single persons like John Hooke, boy servant, and Soloman Prower, man servant to Christopher Martin, a leader of the Strangers. All were buried with no markers on a hill close to the water lest the Indians know how diminished our numbers were.

During the worst part of the disaster, only six or seven healthy adults were fit to care for the sick, doing all the necessary and arduous chores, such as gathering wood and making fires, preparing meat and other victuals, fixing their beds, taking off and washing their filthy clothes, washing their feverish and lice-ridden bodies, and doing all the humble and unmentionable things that sick people need. And they did all this at the risk of their own healthy bodies. I well remember that among these were Elder Brewster and the short, red-faced, red-haired Captain Standish, the hardy soldier who had fought in Holland and who lost his own wife, Rose, to the sickness. There were no Saints and Strangers during this calamitous time, only children of God in deep trouble.

Master Bradford, lying desperately enfeebled in the common house, asked some of the seamen for a drink of beer because the water from the ship was too foul to drink and the brook was frozen. He was told, "Not on your life, not e'en were you me own father." Not long after this the seamen themselves began to fall ill, and half of *them* died as well, yet unlike the passengers, the sailors who were healthy refused to come to the aid of their fellows for fear they themselves would catch the fever. "If they're going to die, they're going to die," they said, and cursed one and another thing (their wives, the other seamen) for causing them to be there. The boatswain, who had been especially evil in his speech and manners to the passengers, fell sick, yet those who on the ship were still healthy nursed him, so that he said, "Oh! you, I now see, show your love like Christians indeed one to another, but we let one another lie and die like dogs."

1620, EARLY RELATIONS WITH THE INDIANS AT NEW PLYMOUTH, FROM THE MEMOIR OF GILES HOPKINS

HAVING SEEN THE Indians in Virginia and had intercourse with them, Father, as I have told you, was chosen to assist with the Indians in many ways. Even before Samoset came to our burgeoning village, I was familiar with their appearance from Father's stories. Soon I could add my own experience to his so that I can say that the Indians of Patuxet (of which Squanto, alas, was the only example), Pokanoket (these are called the Wampanoag), Cape Cod (the Nausets, &c.), Massachusetts, etc., are generally very handsome in appearance, even more so, Father said, than those in Virginia. Samoset himself was from the far north.

They are taller than we English, well-muscled and proportioned, with olive-colored skin, black hair, for the most part, and black eyes. The men generally avoid beards, either because they do not grow well on them or because they prefer to go without the beard. Strangely, some of them wear false beards made from the hair of animals. I have heard it said that one of them offered a sailor with a red beard one of these animal-hair beards because he thought the red beard must be not be his own hair. Some shave their hair atop their heads; others braid it with a part down the middle like those I saw as a child in London. At times they paint their faces black, red, and yellow and beautify their appearance with feathers and shells called wampum; this is especially true of the exalted members such as the sachems and the powwows. The wampum is worn as necklaces and bracelets, which are also made of bone and stone. The women are not so tall, but equally handsome and plump, as are the little boys and girls.

Some think they are white like us only they are made dark because of exposure to the sun and the effects of nature and the oil they like to cover their bodies with. Some say they are remnants of the ten lost tribes of Israel. Yet some of the savages are as dark as the Moors of North Africa (I am told, for I never saw a Moor). Some compare their skin color to that of the gypsies in England.

Be that as it may, they invariably cover their secret parts with animal skins, like Adam and Eve, their women especially being more modest than some of our own. Otherwise, they go naked whenever they can. In the awful cold of the New England winter they wear skins of the various animals that live in their territory: bears, deer, moose, and beaver, and they sometimes truck with tribes from other territories so they can wear skins of animals that are foreign to their own territory. In cold weather they wear the fur side next to their skin; in the warmer weather they do the reverse or remove the fur entirely. Today, of course, they also wear English garments, although many dislike them and often wear them in the same fashion as they wear their animal skins. They dislike English clothes because they find washing them a hard task, having no soap except what they get in trade from the English, and because they can not be certain of having enough to trade to get new clothes when the others are worn out. Though I remember seeing no Irish people in England, I have heard their dress compares to that of the Irish, especially their leathern stockings which attach to their breeches and resemble our boots. For shoes, most of the Indians prefer moose skin, but deer skin, if necessary, suffices for both men and women.

In addition to the necklaces and bracelets I have described, their body decorations are sometimes more permanent. On their cheeks, necks, arms, loins, legs and even the trunks of their bodies they will incise with keen instruments black indelible ink with which they create images of various animals such as those of the wolf, beer, deer, moose, eagle, hawks, &c. I have seen also burned into their skin figures of stars and dots in the form of circles. These they say enhance their physical beauty, but also are part of their religion, each figure being sacred, which I believe and have so been told under promise of secrecy (which I reveal now only because I tell you not my source nor the name of the Indian and tribe I learnt it from). I have other secrets to reveal, my family, secrets about the the darkest, most ignominious ways people may know each other. I am not ready to reveal them yet.

BEFORE SAMOSET CAME to our village or plantation (call it what ye will), one of our members who was hunting fowl saw some dozen Indians a mile or two from our dwellings. He thought he heard voices of many more in the woods. He ran into the village and alarmed everyone so that the men took up their muskets and built a tremendous fire in the place where the Indians were first discovered. In their rush to come after hearing the alarm, Cap. Standish and Francis Cooke left their tools where they had been working in the woods. Returning to retrieve the tools, they found the Indians had stolen them.

From that day it was decided to have Cap. Standish regularly train our men so as to be prepared for any Indian attack. In two years I was old enough to join the men in these exercises. The next day two savages appeared atop the hill and made gestures for the men to come to them. Cap. Standish and my father passed over the brook and approached the savages, laying down the one musket they had brought with them. The savages must have panicked, for they fled back into the woods. It was determined it was time to fortify the hill. To that end the master of the ship and his sailors brought a large cannon called a minion and, together with another piece that was already on the sand, brought them up the hill and mounted them.

That was the 21st of February. On the 3rd of March we heard the pleasing sound of birds singing in the forest. Then we heard the first thunder we had ever heard in America. It was so loud and powerful it seemed as if God Himself was making an announcement, and the rain fell hard and steady for about an hour. How I love these sounds to this day.

On the 16th of March, a fine day, Samoset walked bravely into our village. I will not forget that day, for he was all alone and fearless despite the great alarm his coming had caused. He greeted us in English as if he were an emissary from another world, as indeed he was, being a sachem of or sagamore of Pemaquid Point in what is now called Maine. He told us he had learnt English from the English fishermen at Monchiggon or Monhegan.

You may imagine the many questions the men asked of Samoset. He informed us about the divers sachems and their people surrounding us, how many members they had, and how strong they were. As it was getting windy, somebody offered him the coat of a horseman, for he was naked apart from the leather garment of about nine inches covering his waist. He carried a bow and one arrow with a head and one without. He was taller than any of our men, with black hair hanging down his back, no beard. He asked for beer; we offered strong water instead, together with a buttered biscuit and cheese, some English pudding and duck.

The supper pleased him, and, as 'twere, opened further his mouth. He told us the story of Patuxet, where we now resided, how four years before a great plague had killed all the people living there, which we knew to be true, for there was none to object to our settling this land.

Samoset and our leaders continued talking whilst all the village who were well sat in a circle listening to our ambassador from the savage world. As nightfall approached, however, Gov. Carver and others sought to shake him off by taking him to the ship on our shallop. He was glad to rest there, but the wind arose and the water was too low. Therefore, Gov. Carver and Cap. Standish asked my father if Samoset could spend the night with him in our house.

Whether these arrangements pleased my father I know not. I never asked him. I was thrilled, as ye may imagine. My childish dream from the time we saw the savages in London seemed to be coming true, and how I wished Trevor were with me to share it. The truth was we barely had room in the house, what with four children, my parents, and our two servants. All but my parents slept on the floor, where Samoset had to sleep also. He did not care, nor was there a peep of complaint from anyone else. I do believe we were all in awe. Father and mother treated Samoset as an honored guest, offering food and drink (bread and beer was all we had, and some dried meat). I got to sleep next to him and smell his musky, woodsy smell and accidentally touch his hard arms. He fell asleep straightaway, but I could not sleep for hours imagining the adventures he must have had and that I too might one day experience.

BEFORE RETURNING TO the great sachem of the Wampanoags, Massasoit, the following morning, Samoset was given a ring, a bracelet, and a knife. He said he would bring back with him some of the Wampanoags and beaver furs to trade with us.

He returned the very next day, which was the Sabbath, accompanied by five other Indians, tall like himself, and wearing deer skins except for the most important of them, who wore the skin of a wild cat over his arm. Otherwise, they were in appearance much as I have described. We asked that they leave their bows and arrows outside the village limits, and they complied. We offered food and sang a pious song for them. In return they sang and danced for us. I heard Francis Cooke call them clowns, but their music and dancing was to me, a boy of fourteen, like almost everything else about them: thrilling. I got up to join them, but Mother pulled my arm and I sat down. They brought in a little leather case some powdered corn which, when mixed with water, is good to eat. Also they brought some tobacco, which they smoked from finely carved wooden pipes with faces of men or figures of animals on the ends where the tobacco is inserted.

Although they had brought some skins, Gov. Carver refused to trade, perhaps because it was the Sabbath. He told them to bring more and then we would truck with them. At that time they produced all the tools that had been stolen in the woods and returned them. The governor told them this was our holy day and they departed, all but Samoset, who said he was ill. Some believed he was pretending in order that he could continue his stay with us, and he did, until Wednesday.

All this time I helped the men plow the ground and plant our seeds. Governor Carver and others met to outline the rules to govern the colony as agreed in the compact signed by my father and others on the ship. And our carpenter, who had been taken with the general sickness-- scurvy they thought it was--finished his repairs on our shallop and the last of those living on the ship were brought ashore.

On the 22nd of March, another fair day, Samoset returned with Squanto, of whom ye already know. They told us they had brought with them the great sachem or sagamore Massasoit and his brother, Quadequina. They and about sixty of their men waited in the nearby forest. The leaders were unwilling to send Governor Carver to them, and they were unwilling to send Massasoit and Quadequina to us. Squanto agreed to be our ambassador, as he would do so often in the future. The Indians agreed to receive one of our company, and Edward Winslow was chosen.

Master Winslow presented to Massasoit two knives and a chain made of copper and a jewel. He gave Quadequina a knife and an earring made of a precious stone. Together with these tokens, Master Winslow brought some strong water, biscuits, and butter, all very much appreciated. He told them that all we desired was to truck with them in peace, that our King James greeted him lovingly and peacefully and welcomed him as a friend and ally.

Master Winslow was decked in his armor and sword, and after he had eaten and drunk with the sachem and his brother, Massasoit expressed a wish to buy both the armor and the sword (so Master Winslow told my father, who later told me). This Master Winslow gently refused.

Through our interpreter, Squanto, Massasoit presented his plan. Our ambassador would remain with his brother, Quadequina, as a token of our good will, and he, Massasoit, would parley with our governor, taking with him twenty of his men, unarmed. We agreed on the condition we keep a half dozen of the Indians.

As ye know, my children, Quadequina was to become the father-in-law of my wife's father and therefore my wife, Catherine's grandfather, so you will not be surprised to become acquainted with the fact that I would dearly love to know--as I assume would you--what conversation was had between Master Winslow and Quadequina. I am sorry to have to say this I can not provide.

What I can provide, however, is a first-hand description from a book I have been privileged to obtain. It was printed in London in 1622, not long after the events I am writing about took place, and it was called *A Relation or Journal of the beginning and proceedings of the English Plantation settled at Plymouth in NEW ENGLAND, by certain English Adventurers both Merchants and others. With their difficult passage, their safe arrival, their joyful building of, and comfortable planting themselves in the now well defended town of NEW PLYMOUTH, &c.* The friend who procured this volume for me said with some assurance, and I agree with him, that the principal authors are Edward Winslow and William Bradford.

Now you may ask why do I not provide my own description of these our native friends and relations. My answer is that I can and will give you my boy's impressions. They were colored, as ye may guess, by my infatuation with the natives of our country. I saw both Massasoit and Quadequina as larger than perhaps they were. Their bodies gleamed, probably from the oil the Indians typically rub all over themselves for protection in both cold and hot weather. They reminded me of nothing less than grown-up versions of David in the Bible who, if they were so disposed, could easily have destroyed our little colony. But they were, unlike David, bigger, taller, better proportioned than any of our leaders, particularly Cap. Myles Standish, who stood like a dwarf next to them, though he was never a dwarf in spirit. To be truthful, I wanted to worship these giants who seemed to come out of the romances I had heard of or read from olden times.

Here is the description of Massasoit and his men:

In his person he was a very lusty man, in his best years, an able body, grave of countenance, and spare of speech. In his attire little or nothing differing from the rest of his followers, only in a great chain of white bone beads about his neck, and at it behind his neck hangs a little bag of tobacco, which he drank and gave us to drink; his face was painted with a

sad red like murry, and oiled both head and
face, that he looked greasily. All his followers
likewise, were in their face, in part or in whole
painted, some black, some red, some yellow,
and some white, some with crosses, and other
antic works; some had skins on them, and some
naked, all strong, tall, all men in appearance.

When Quadequina came to join the others in the village, he
was afeared of our musketry and the men followed his
request that they be put aside. The same book describes him
thus:

He was a proper tall young man, of a
very modest and seemly countenance, and he
did kindly like of our entertainment, so we
conveyed him likewise as we did the king, but
divers of their people stayed still.

The author (or authors) of the book write further: "One thing
I forgot, the king had in his bosom, hanging in a string, a
great long knife; he marvelled much at our trumpet, and some
of his men would sound it as well as they could."

Before they departed into the forest, leaving Samoset
and Squanto with us in the village, we had the following
agreement signed by Massasoit and Gov. Carver (the words
come from the selfsame book):

1. That neither he nor any of his should
injure or do hurt to any of our people.

2. And if any of his did hurt to any of ours,
he should send the offender, that we might punish
him.

3. That if any of our tools were taken away
when our people were at work, he should cause them

to be restored, and if ours did any harm to any of his, we would do the like to them.

    4. If any did unjustly war against him, we would aid him; if any did war against us, he should aid us.

    5. He should send to his neighbor confederates, to certify them of this, that they might not wrong us, but might be likewise comprised in the conditions of peace.

    6. That when their men came to us, they should leave their bows and arrows behind them, as we should do our pieces when we came to them.

    Lastly, that doing thus, King James would esteem of him as his friend and ally.

Whether intentionally or not, this peace agreement or treaty was unequal against the Indians, for it does not provide for "us" not to "injure or do hurt to" them, and if we did, nothing says we should deliver the offender to *them*.

Lastly, we are not required to tell any Europeans not to harm them, though they must require their "neighbor confederates" not to "wrong us."

    My children and others who may read this, know that I am no heathen. Although I was never a Separatist or Puritan, I have always been a Christian and striven to live by the principles of our Lord. Therefore, I am pained to have to set down here how we Englishmen behaved toward our aboriginal brothers and sisters, particularly since ye are blood of their blood and I am not personally guiltless concerning these matters.

CHAPTER THREE
PLYMOUTH COLONY'S EQUIVOCAL
RELATIONSHIPS WITH THE INDIANS,
THE FURTHER HISTORY OF STEPHEN HOPKINS,
THE ABORTIVE COLONIES OF
WESSAGUSETT AND MERRY MOUNT,
OTHER ASPECTS OF EARLY PLYMOUTH,
BOTH RELIGIOUS & OTHERWISE

29 MARCH 1864, EASTHAM, CAPE COD

GILES HOPKINS HAS alluded to a rumor which has persisted in my family for generations. I mean the rumor that we have Wampanoag blood. Despite the objections of my dearly beloved late aunt, I am interested to read how this came about, in his opinion (and who would know better than he?), and whether his story would stand up in a court of historians. Aunt Huldah, as I have noted, and many others in the family, were not pleased to think they might have Indian blood.

I wonder, also, whether the "darkest, most ignominous ways people may know each other" might have anything to do with Aunt Huldah's now almost nightly visitations. I almost welcome them as a direct contact with her, better than those offered by the Spiritualists in Boston. But good heavens! Surely she can not be referring to the abominations of the flesh condemned in both Leviticus and in the Apostle Paul's Epistle to the Romans! If that is so, her bitter prejudice need not be my own. Or should it be?

REGARDING THE AFOREMENTIONED rumor, I recall reading an article in *Putnam's Magazine* a few years ago the anonymous writer's opinion that Cape Codders have redder faces than any of those in the country because they are all sunburned Britons. The Indians at Marshpee, he wrote, were also red, but some have faces "smutted" (I remember that was the exact word he used) by a bit of Negro blood. I recall writing to the editor of the magazine regarding his racial prejudice. By then I was a known abolitionist, and that fact the editor used to dismiss my disagreement with the author's use of the word "smutted."

The article was in plain error when it stated that on Cape Cod there was otherwise no "mixture of races." My family alone, if the rumor proves true, as I believe it will, refutes this statement.

And just last week I was enjoying some clam chowder at a local establishment when I made the acquaintance of a steer man on a lobster boat. True enough, his face was of a deep red color. He was weather-worn, with a bag under his right eye, and hair flying out from under his black seaman's hat. He spoke of his Wampanoag father, who was a "chief," he said. Whether or not that was true, I could tell he was not a full-blooded Englishman by any means.

My nephew, Paul, agreed with me. A charming, handsome boy in the bloom of early manhood, Paul had just turned sixteen, and I invited him to come to stay with me for a few days. Having to entertain Paul was an attractive change from my usual routine, particularly my labors on the papers. He is a reader, like me, and enjoys nature walks such as Thoreau made on Cape Cod. We particularly enjoyed the beach, which they say has not changed since our ancestors arrived. Paul likes to identify the many sea birds that fly this way.

Now that we are free from Aunt Huldah's reproving eyes, we read together, aloud by turns, not only the tales of Poe, Hawthorne, and Dickens and the essays of Emerson and Thoreau, but also the poetry of Poe, and that of Longfellow, Whittier, and, from across the sea, Keats, Shelley, Byron—ah, too many to mention. We love the sentiment and thought of Tennyson's *In Memoriam* and the wonderful, and may I say unique, poetry of Walt Whitman in his *Leaves of Grass*, and especially his *Song of Myself* and his *Calamus* poems contained therein. Here is a favorite of mine:

> Recorders ages hence,
> Come, I will take you down underneath this
> > impassive exterior, I will tell you what to
> > say of me,
> Publish my name and hang up my picture as
> > that of the tenderest lover,
> The friend the lover's portrait, of whom his
> > friend his lover was fondest,
> Who was not proud of his songs but of the
> > measureless ocean of love within him,
> > and freely pour'd it forth,
> Who often walk'd lonesome walks thinking of
> > his dear friends, his lovers,
> Who pensive away from one he lov'd often lay
> > sleepless and dissatisfied at night,
> Who knew too well the sick, sick dread lest the
> > one he lov'd might secretly be
> > indifferent to him.
> Whose happiest days were far away through
> > fields, in woods, on hills, he and

another wandering hand in hand, they
twain apart from other men,
Who oft as he saunter'd the streets curv'd with
his arm the shoulder of his friend, while
the arm of his friend rested upon him
also.

Aunt Huldah would never approve of a verse such as this,
nor would my ancestor, yet it is neither dark nor ignominious,
but wholesome, like the love I share with my dear nephew,
Paul. Did Aunt Huldah confuse his name with that of the
author of Romans? Nonsense. The very idea is ridiculous.

Now I am getting off my topic again. I return to Giles's
memoir:

1621, NEW PLYMOUTH, STEPHEN HOPKINS AND THE INDIANS, FROM THE MEMOIR OF GILES HOPKINS

FATHER WAS AGAIN called upon as an emissary to the
Indians. He and Edward Winslow were sent to Pokanoket, as
the country where Massasoit resided was called. The leaders
of the colony, Gov. Carver, William Bradford (who would
take his place as governor in April after Carver took sick and
died), Isaac Allerton, Cap. Standish, etc., desired to know
what Pokanoket was like, how far away it was, how many
warriors were under Massasoit's direct command, and
whether we could establish some rules as to their coming to
visit us. Also, they wanted to make good on any slights the
Indians may have felt we had done unto them.

Father and Master Winslow took Squanto as
interpreter, and as a gift to Massasoit they brought an
Englishman's red horseman's coat made of cotton and
trimmed with white lace. The coat was a token of the

colony's desire for continued peace and friendship. Another part of their message was to tell them we would welcome a return visit but as our harvest was uncertain, we could not entertain a company so large as he had hitherto brought with him. Also, we wished that those Indians on Cape Cod from which we took the corn be told that we were ready to recompense them whenever we could. Because they must be our enemies for what we had done, it would be better for the Pokanokets to be our emissaries to them.

Father told me they passed country that, like Patuxet, looked abandoned, as if people had lived there recently. Indeed, there were villages empty of living people with the bones of dead ones lying on the ground, which betokened either there were too many dead to bury or that all had died, leaving no one to bury them. Yet, Father said, the countryside was rich with sundry trees, such as cedar, pine, oak, sassafras, and beech, and fruit, such as raspberries, plums, cherries, gooseberries, and strawberries, and fish, such as salmon, trout, eels, and giant sturgeon, which be ugly but very good to eat. Those Indians who had survived provided them with whatever food they had and Father and Master Winslow gave them beads in return.

"Are all the natives of this country as friendly as ye?" Winslow asked.

"No, no," they said through Squanto. "The Narragansetts, who live across the water, they be our enemies."

"This we knew," Father told me and the others in our house. It was one of the reasons Massasoit was so eager to have us as allies.

"When we arrived at the village of Massasoit," Father said, "we were fed oysters and divers kinds of fish. Massasoit was not there, and one of his warriors went for him. As soon as we heard he was coming, Squanto suggested we fire our muskets. My companion, having prepared his piece and raising it to discharge, all the women and children became afeared and dashed away, making many noises, and would not be quieted until we set our pieces down.

"When Massasoit came, we fired our muskets in his honor. He welcomed us and, after Squanto had relayed the import of our visit and we had given him the red horseman's coat, he put it on along with the jeweled, copper chain we had also given him and disported himself proudly before his people, who were in awe at his apparel.

"He agreed with our requests, promising to prevent his warriors from disturbing us and to give us corn seed. Then he again displayed himself much as doth our own king and noblemen, and his men yelled their approval. He uttered something in their tongue and they answered (so said Squanto): 'Yes, you are our king and we are your men. We will be at peace with these Englishmen and sell our furs to them.' Massasoit continued, naming about thirty different Indian villages, receiving the same answer each time so that we grew weary alistening.

"Then we sat down to smoke tobacco, and Massasoit began a conversation about England and the majesty of King James and his court. That the king continued living without a wife for over a year after his first wife had died was a wonder to him. 'You must not let the French go to the Narragansett now that this country belongs to King James,' he warned us. He said he was sorry he had no food for us, having interrupted his hunting to come to us.

"It being late, we asked if we might sleep. He was glad to let us sleep on his own bed, we two on one end, he and his wife on the other. The bed was made of long boards and thin mats about a foot from the floor. Since the ground could hold no more, two of his men joined us on the bed. I could not sleep but an hour or two what with the crushing in of bodies and the lice and fleas and the singing that led to their own sleep, not to mention the mosquitoes!

"The next day many of the sachems who ruled under Massasoit came to visit us along with their braves. They loved to play games of chance and skill for knives and skins, shooting their bows and arrows at a mark, so we offered to do the same with our pieces for some skins, but they were afeared, asking only that we fire at the mark. I shot with hail-shot, and they were amazed to see so many holes on the mark.

"At about noon Massasoit returned with some fishes he himself had shot. Two of these were sufficient to serve about forty men. This was the only food we had since our arrival there, and though Massasoit nearly begged us to stay, we excused ourselves, saying we had to be back to observe the Sabbath. Our strength was ebbing for fatigue from the sleeping conditions and the unending talk and singing.

"Massasoit was ashamed to have so little to give us by way of food, but we passed that off. He kept Squanto as an emissary to various places to get trade for us and sent with us in his stead Tokamahamon, whom we already knew.

"Coming back with some other men Massasoit sent with us, we stopped at a village we had before stopped at and were given some parched corn and some seafood. We each drank a pipe of tobacco as well. Other villages offered similar generosities. Yet on the way one of Massasoit's men stole some victuals and left us. Only later did he find us again and was disturbed that we gave him nothing. After telling him why we disapproved of him, we offered him a few beads and a bit of tobacco, this before a large group of savages. The man offered us some parched corn, but Edward Winslow did tell him 'we would not receive that which was stolen upon any terms; if we did, our God would be angry with us, and destroy us.'

"Yea, I know Winslow's words are not congruous with our own thievery regarding the corn we had taken on Cape Cod. Perhaps he wished to convey a lesson unto the savages. I did not ask him."

Hearing his report on his mission to the great Massasoit, my father seemed himself like a hero to me.

BY MID-1621 ALL the surviving passengers aboard the *Mayflower* were settled in the plantation, and it was much easier to keep the Sabbath as required by custom and the law. Once the fort and meeting house was built, we customarily marched to the services, starting at Cap. Standish's house, called there by the beating of a drum. We dressed in our humdrum, uncomfortable black clothes, so different from our colorful weekday apparel, with Sabbath-day hats and cloaks, which would make us look like clowns were we not dressed so darkly and so alike each other. The men and older boys held their muskets, always on guard against wild beasts or savages. Three together, we followed whoever was selected the sergeant, with the governor behind us, wearing his lengthy robe, the preacher on his right, and the captain on his left carrying his pistols and a little cane. During the service, each who had a piece placed it beside him on the ground.

Since we had no ordained minister at this time, Elder Brewster served as our preacher. Having never recorded his sermons, I can only relate from memory the main points of a sermon that has stayed with me all these years. It was one of his three-hour speeches before the congregation, of which he gave two each Sabbath.

I remember his text, Psalm 2, taken from the Geneva Bible used by the Separatists. I use a copy borrowed from a friend:

1. Why doe the heathen rage, and the people murmure in vaine?

2. The kings of the earth band themselves, and the princes are assembled together against the Lord, and against his Christ.

3. Let us breake their bands, and cast their cordes from us.

4. But he that dwelleth in the heaven, shal laugh: the Lord shall have them in derision.

5. Then shall hee speake unto them in his wrath, and vexe them in his sore displeasure, saying,

6. Even I have set my King upon Zion mine holy mountaine.

7. I will declare the decree: that is, the Lord hath said unto me, Thou art my sonne: this day have I begotten thee.

8. Aske of me, and I shal give thee the heathen for thine inheritance, and the ends of the earth for thy possession.

9. Thou shalt crush them with a scepter of iron, and breake them in pieces like a potters vessell.

10. Be wise now therefore, ye kings: bee learned ye judges of the earth.

11. Serve the Lord in feare and rejoyce in trembling.

12. Kisse the sonne, lest he be angry, and ye perish in the way, when his wrath shal suddenly burne, blessed are all that trust in him.

These, in the main, are Elder Brewster's comments on this scripture. "We have," he said, "been called as a people chosen of God to establish His kingdom in a land of heathens, savages both uncivilized and cruel, who roam the earth with no dignity and little or no labor to cultivate the land God has made for the subjugation of man, people who 'rage' and 'murmur in vaine,' as the scripture says, people who 'band themselves' and gather 'together against the Lord,' and, yea, 'against his Christ,' as our Lord and Savior Jesus Christ is here prefigured in the psalm.

"We have heard their savage cries and their dancing unto the devil, whom they serve. We have observed how their men do wear their long hair in a womanish manner, diverting themselves from the ordinance of Almighty God as to the deportment of the sexes.

"As the psalm saith, God shall 'vexe them in his sore displeasure.' And we, my brothers and sisters in the Lord, are the instruments of God's will here in the country he has given us. That our Plymouth should have been settled on land disinhabited by pestilence and disease is a sign that we are meant to inherit it, as the scripture says: 'Aske of me, and I shal give thee the heathen for thine inheritance, and the ends of the earth for thy possession.'

"For the moment it is prudent to be kind to these people and, if they so wish it, bring them to the Lord. But if they turn their backs on the divine mission to which we are called, the Lord God gives us leave, yea He commands us to 'crush them with a scepter of iron, and breake them in pieces like a potters vessell.'

"All of us, be we those who have suffered the persecution of that false king of England and have had to sojourn for a time in an odious foreign country and had to leave the comfort of our pastors, Richard Clyfton and John Robinson, and have now come to the New World, or be ye those who were formerly 'strangers' amongst us,--all of us I say must now carry out the will of our Holy Father in heaven to, as the psalm enjoins, 'Serve the Lord in feare and rejoyce in trembling.'

"Yeah, 'Kisse the sonne,' the Lord Jesus Christ, lest He be angry and we 'perish in the way' under His burning wrath. 'Blessed are all that trust in him,' saith the Lord.

"We may have many hardships ahead, but be diligent to follow God's word and will and we can not help but triumph!"

And on he went, describing how we had overcome our enemies, the heathen Indians, and come to what he made sound like a paradise on earth made especially for us, the "chosen people," by which he meant those who followed the word of the Pastors Clyfton and Robinson.

Were it not for my father's wise guidance, I think my sister Constance and I would have endeavored to become members of the Puritan church. Now in my elder years, I am glad neither of us did that.

5 APRIL 1864, EASTHAM, CAPE COD

MANY OF THE HISTORICAL facts Giles refers to are fairly well known to the public. The people he calls Separatists or Puritans most people today call "Pilgrims." I have before me an article which illustrates my point and which I saved. It is by the editor of *The Ladies' Repository* (the editor's name, I happen to know from my connections in publishing circles, is D. W. Clark). Published just a few years ago in 1858, the article declares that

> The history of the Pilgrim Fathers is a part of the history of our country--to be read and re-read by each successive generation. No matter, then, how often the story is repeated, or in how many ways and forms it is published. If we would kindle a stern and abiding love of liberty in the breasts of American youth, let them study not merely the Declaration of Independence and the chivalric deeds of the Revolution, but also the history of the Pilgrim Fathers. That history, as it embodies the very marrow of religious and civil liberty, will impart the strength and beauty of its principles to the youthful mind.

This little passage tells me two things. One, my own history (or, rather, that of Giles Hopkins and the other writers of these Plymouth Papers) ought to be welcomed by the general public and, in particular, the youth of America. And two, D. W. Clark has little idea of what he is talking about if he thinks the "Pilgrims" granted religious and civil liberty to the Indians or to those of other religious persuasions. This I know even without benefit of my ancestors' memoirs.

In any case, Giles does not use the term "Pilgrim," and, I think, he is right. They are not called Pilgrims in the historical papers he refers to, at least not to my knowledge.

OUR PRESIDENT LINCOLN just last year proclaimed Thanksgiving a holiday each November, following the day of Thanksgiving in August to remember the Battle of Gettysburg, so I had hoped Giles, Pilgrim or not, would give credit to his fellows for the first Thanksgiving in 1621 with the Indians. All he writes is that after their first harvest was over, the governor ordered some men to hunt and bring in some waterfowl which, added to their vegetables, made a great feast. The few Indians already with them, probably Hobbamock, his wives, and their family of about ten, and Squanto, were joined by the mighty Massasoit and about ninety of his men. They came because a messenger had run to tell the great sachem about the musket shots the Plymouth people had discharged in celebration. Perhaps they were afraid the settlers were preparing to attack them. Who knows? Realizing this was a celebration to give thanks, not a war party, Massasoit sent out some of his men to hunt, and they brought back five deer for the three-day celebration. That is about all Giles writes, not much more than what may be found in the book called *Mourt's Relation*.

Ah yes, except that Giles says they did have some wild turkey and fish, and he does mention Hobbamock, who lived near the Plymouth people, and Squanto, who lived with them and had as much to do as any other Indian in saving the colony from starvation. He taught them how to plant corn and fertilize the plants with fish. The Indian corn grew better than any of the English crop seed brought over on the *Mayflower*.

I NOTICE GILES also briefly describes the second marriage of Governor William Bradford, which occurred two years later, in 1623. The governor's first wife, you will recall, died after falling off the *Mayflower* at what is today

Provincetown. Mr. Bradford's second wife, Alice Southworth, herself a widow, came over on the ship *Anne* not long before their marriage. The great sachem, Massasoit, was invited and of his five wives he brought only one, along with four minor sachems and about one hundred and twenty warriors armed with bows and arrows, which, after the colonists greeted them by shooting their firearms in the air, they happily deposited in the house of the governor.

Massasoit's contribution to the feast was several deer and a wild turkey. He and his party entertained the colonists with their own native dances and loud singing that seems to have so astounded and annoyed the Englishmen. Curiously, one of the adventurers, Emmanuel Altham, who was then visiting Plymouth, demanded a handsome young boy of about fifteen years of age, whom he said he wished to give to his brother in England, Sir Edward Altham. Massasoit flatly refused him.

ABOUT A YEAR after the first thanksgiving celebration, that is in 1622, Squanto died from a mysterious illness. He had been taken captive by a minor sachem, Corbitant, who was under the authority of Massasoit but suspected to be making an alliance with the Narragansetts. An amusing incident occurred when the men who went to fetch him (among them Stephen Hopkins) accidentally fired one of their "pieces," as they called their firearms. The boys in the encampment where they happened to be, pretended to be females, believing the English did not harm women. They beseeched the men, saying "*Neen squaes,*" meaning "I am a woman." They were not harmed.

This is not the first time Giles Hopkins mentions a confusion of the sexes. On the aforementioned trip to visit

Massasoit, Stephen Hopkins noticed a conspicuously masculine person among the Indian warriors, who, upon closer inspection, had all the physical traits of a woman. Stephen told his family about this unusual person by way of illustration, a joke as it were about how different the Indians could be from the English.

The men found Squanto, but before reaching Plymouth, he fell ill, bleeding profusely from his nose, a sign, the Indians said, that he would surely die. And he did. Before dying, however, he asked Gov. Bradford, who had taken the place of a sick Captain Standish on this expedition, to pray that he would go to the Englishmen's heaven and to their God there. Squanto must be counted as the first, and one of the very few, converts of the first generation of Plymouth settlers.

Squanto's death was timely for him because Massasoit had discovered Squanto was threatening to get the English to make war on him. Squanto also said he knew where the English had buried the plague and that he could get them to use it against the Pokanoket whenever he desired. Massasoit sent his own knife to the governor so that he might behead Squanto, but Gov. Bradford, though he admitted the righteousness of Massasoit's decision, was loath to lose his interpreter and helper. So he delayed doing anything till God in His good time was pleased to take Squanto, or so Bradford might have said.

NOW GILES TURNS to an episode not taught in the schools when the story of our "Pilgrim Fathers" is told. In this time of bloody war between the North and the South, perhaps this episode will seem but a minor blemish in the history of the first English colony. Nevertheless, Giles clearly thinks it worth recording, and so do I. Here is my transcript:

1623, PLYMOUTH AND WESSAGUSETT, FROM THE MEMOIR OF GILES HOPKINS

DURING THE WINTER and spring of 1623, when I had reached the age of sixteen, Mr. Weston, formerly one of our adventurers, sent two ships, the *Charity* and the *Swan*, to found a new colony at Wessagusett, in the country occupied by the Massachusett Indians. Almost to a man the settlers were indolent, expecting I know not how to live after their hasty use of their supplies.

They began to steal from the Indians and to their great disgrace divers of them became their servants, fetching water and such for them, only to get a little corn to eat. So desperate were they, some of them sold the very clothing on their backs for food. As they had lost their spiritual strength, so they lost their moral and bodily strength. Indeed, I heard from John Cooke that one of them had so lost his health that whilst he hunted for shellfish he got caught in the mud and was found dead in the very spot.

The Indians no longer respected the Englishmen and began to make sport of them. To give an example, the men would fill their baskets with shellfish or some roots they had found, and when the baskets were full, the Indians would deprive the poor souls of their food by taking the baskets from them. To regain the good will of the Indians (and some food, they hoped) these desperate men went so far as to hang one of their own who had stolen corn from the Indians.

While this was happening, Master Winslow and Hobbamock had gone to Massasoit, who was so sick no one expected him to live. His large *wetu*, i.e., his wigwam, was crowded with his family and all the minor sachems under his authority, and whoever else could find a space. The powwow was making incantations over him without any visible results, but Winslow, with the aid of herbs, English physics, and prayer brought him back. Then, as if in recompense, Massasoit warned him that the outlying tribes, the Massachusetts and others, were intending to attack them because of the weakness and thievery of the Englishmen at Wessagusett and his own sickness, which made it impossible for him to do battle.

Hearing this news by means of a runner, and, as he thought having it confirmed by an Englishman come from Wessagusett, Gov. Bradford waited till Winslow returned, and then dispatched him with Cap. Standish and seven other men, along with Hobbamock, to go to Wessagusett and vanquish the enemy. The governor said he durst not send more for fear the Indians may suspect their purpose and the mission would come to naught. My Father, I am happy to tell you, was not among the party because he was awaiting the birth of my brother, Caleb, born during the middle of March. I learnt the story from Hobbamock's son, Waban, meaning "wind" in their language, who by then had become my friend. His father was a witness, not a party to the assassinations.

He said that when the Plymouth men arrived at Wessagusett, Standish and Winslow were shocked to find the Englishmen of the colony standing about among the Indians with no fear and some of them doing chores for the Indians. Wituwamet and Pecksuot, both far taller than Standish and the most vehement of the Indians, made bold to say they were not afraid of the Englishmen, as did Wituwamet's brother, only eighteen years of age.

The party, led by Cap. Standish, waited two days to assess the situation. Standish gathered, through Hobbamock, that the Massachusetts, notwithstanding the bravado of Wituwamet, his young brother, and Pecksuot, restrained themselves from killing the English settlers for fear the men at Patuxet would come and kill them and their squaw sachem. On the third day, under pretense of wanting to feast and parley about trade with them, Cap. Standish enticed Wituwamet and Pecksuot and two other Massachusetts, one of them being the brother of Wituwamet, into joining him and his fellows in a wigwam. A scuffle ensued, six or seven against four. The Englishmen forced the Indians' knives from them, slit their throats and stabbed them in their guts, killing all but Wituwamet's brother.

Cap. Standish tied the young man's hands behind his back and forced him out into the open. There he strung a rope with a noose over the branch of a tree, placed the noose around the young warrior's neck, and with the help of two other men hoisted him in the air, swung him to and fro and then let go, leaving him to hang to death. Although the hanging did not break his neck and he suffered a terrible choking, the young man never made a murmur of complaint. He made no grimace; his visage was unmoved, like those of the Stoics of ancient Greece.

Before Standish and his men left the degenerate colony, he and his men murdered three more Massachusett Indians. Later several of the Wessagusett Englishmen were caught in the woods and killed in retaliation by the Massachusetts.

Hobbamock, who was a *pniece,* a kind of holy counselor and warrior, had till now done nothing but watch with sickness in his heart. But then he and the Standish party came across the company of the Massachusett warrior, Obtakiest, who was bent on revenge. When the two sides began to exchange shots, Hobbamock boldly stepped into the middle of the battle, and both sides quit their shooting, Obtakiest because he feared a *pniece* of the Pokanoket after his own *pnieces* had proved vulnerable in battle, and Standish because Hobbamock was his man and the interpreter of Plymouth Plantation.

Cap. Standish contented himself with bringing the head of Wituwamet back to the plantation and putting it on a pike by the opening to the fort, also used for our Sabbath meetings, as a rebuke to any Indian who might dare oppose our people. It had been several years since as a child I had seen the heads of criminals on pikes in London. That did not make my stomach any less queasy. I ran to the fence and vomited, my heart sick with grief that our own people had been so evil to our neighbors. I never spoke again with Mr. Standish save when I had to.

Neither was the revered pastor of the Separatists, the Rev. John Robinson, pleased with these murders, for I have it from John Cooke he wrote against the slaughter of these unfortunate Indians and wished that his flock had won them to the Gospel before killing any of them. Father said that if any should have been punished it was Weston's men for provoking the Indians. If ever I had considered converting to the Separatist church, this barbarity changed my thinking forever. Yet, as I shall reveal in good time, I am not guiltless myself.

MY CHILDREN AND grandchildren, compared to the injustices done unto the Massachusett Indians, many incidents in our own family may seem somewhat trivial. But since I write this especially for ye, I will relate divers of the events that may be of interest if only to reveal the characters, both good and not, of my father, myself, and others. You will not think all the events I relate trivial.

BUT TO CONTINUE I should tell ye that the first division of the land occurred in this same year, 1623. Until then all land was held in common and in that respect only did we resemble the earliest Christians, who held all things in common. My father, owing to the size of his household, was given a goodly amount of property, six acres. Hobbamock's land lay between that of my father and that of John Howland, just outside the palisade.

We children, both the older ones, like me, almost a man, and the boys and girls no longer clinging to their mothers, had to work every day, apart from the Sabbath, as ye know. We older boys had to help build and maintain our houses and hunt and fish. We helped to plow the fields. The younger boys watched the fields of Indian corn, barley, wheat, and rye to make sure no crows would eat the seeds or dogs or wolves would devour the fish we had planted for fertilizer. After two weeks the fishes would be rotten and danger of this was past, but always we had to beware of wolves and bears attacking our animals. For the fields, the boys had stones to throw at any intruders; otherwise, we had to keep our pieces handy in case of beast or Indian attack, which latter event never happened at Plymouth. The women planted the corn with their little boys and girls beside them. Each house had its own private plots, oblong and outlined with stones, for household gardens, and these were tended by the women and children also.

All the women and children helped to shuck the corn and prepare the other crops. Rye, for example, had to be cut and wrapped into sheaves, which were then stacked and left to dry in the fields. Threshing was next. We had to beat the stalks till the little grains tumbled out. To remove the skin covering the grain, winnowing was done by the women using a large and shallow basket. As they tossed the grain the skin coverings fell away. Next the women, boys, and girls used a mortar and pestle to grind the grain, making it into flour. We saved the straw for thatching roofs, stuffing beds, and spreading on the ground for the chickens, goats, sheep, pigs, and cows.

15 April 1864, Eastham, Cape Cod

THE EVENTS IN the next section of Giles Hopkins's memoirs have been recorded in Mr. Hawthorne's exemplary "twice-told tale," entitled "The Maypole of Merry Mount." It is strange how the history of this aberrant colony in the early years of New England has gotten hold of the imagination of so many Americans. "Bright were the days at Merry Mount, when the Maypole was the banner staff of that gay colony!" Hawthorne begins his tale.

Since discovering the papers of Giles Hopkins, I have been collecting whatever books and other antiquities I can on the period in which he lived. One of the books I was so fortunate to find at a shop in Boston that specializes in antiquarian books is called *New English Canaan*, by Thomas Morton himself, the instigator of Merry Mount colony's excesses and a former member of that other, earlier aberrant colony at Wessagusett.

C. 1625-1628, MERRYMOUNT

Morton writes this of his maypole:

> The Inhabitants of Passonagessit
> (having translated the name of their habitation
> from that ancient savage name to Merrymount;
> and being resolved to have the new name
> confirmed for a memorial to after-ages) did
> devise amongst themselves to have it performed
> in a solemn manner with revels, and merriment
> after the old English custom: prepared to set up
> a Maypole upon the festival of Philip and Jacob;
> and therefore brewed a barrel of excellent beer,
> and provided a case of bottles to be spent, with
> other good cheer, for all comers of that day. . . .
> And upon May Day they brought the Maypole
> to the place appointed, with drums, guns,
> pistols, and other fitting instruments, for that
> purpose; and there erected it with the help of
> savages, that came thither of purpose to see the
> manner of our revels.

Morton then describes the maypole: "A goodly pine tree 80 foot long, was reared up, with a pair of buck's horns nailed on, somewhat near unto the top of it: where it stood as a fair sea-mark for directions, how to find out the way to Mine Host of Merrymount." "Mine Host" is, I need not emphasize, Morton himself. And he recorded the poem he created and posted on the maypole itself ("Rise Oedipus, and if thou canst unfold"). He also wrote a "merry song," which the party sang in a chorus with a soloist, who "filled out the good liquor like Ganymede and Jupiter," as they danced "hand in hand about the maypole." The song is too long to quote, but here are the first four lines:

> Drink and be merry, merry, merry boys,
> Let all your delight be in Hymen's joys,
> Io to Hymen now the day is come,
> About the merry maypole take a room.

Whether Mr. Hawthorne had Morton's text when he wrote his tale I know not. He gives as his authority "Strutt's Book of English Sports and Pastimes" and, vaguely, "the grave pages of our New England annalists," so I doubt he had read Morton, whose pages are anything but "grave."

Perhaps it is better thus, for the romance writer embellishes the maypole with "a silken banner, colored like the rainbow," streaming from "its top." To the banner he adds green boughs, "some with silvery leaves, fastened by ribbons that fluttered in fantastic knots of twenty different colors . . . Garden flowers, and blossoms of the wilderness," etc.

Morton bewails the fact that "The setting up of this maypole was a lamentable spectacle to the precise Separatists: that lived at New Plymouth. They termed it an idol; yea they called it the Calf of Horeb: and stood at defiance with the place, naming it Mount Dagon; threatening to make it a woeful mount and not a merry mount." The Separatists named the place after the Philistine god, Dagon, but Gov. Bradford, in his history, *Of Plymouth Plantation,* writes, "So they or others now changed the name of their place again and called it Mount Dagon." Who are we to believe?

Let Giles tell the story:

A year or two after the massacre at Wessagusett, another colony attempted to grow roots in Massachusetts of which our Separatist leaders disapproved. This was Mount

Wollaston, named after the captain of the ship who brought the settlers there, most of them indentured servants. When the captain proposed taking the passengers to Virginia and selling the indentures to colonists there, a Mr. Thomas Morton persuaded some few of them to stay with him at the place he renamed Merrymount. Having sent his spies to Merrymount, Gov. Bradford reported that the men had fallen into "great licentiousness and led a dissolute life, pouring out themselves into all profaneness." Morton had "set up a maypole, drinking and dancing about it many days together, inviting the Indian women for their consorts, dancing and frisking together like so many fairies, or furies, rather; and worse practices." I believe those are his exact words.

Our governor's spies were particularly adept, for they discovered, I assume whilst the members of the party were sleeping after their revelries, poems and songs stuck onto the maypole, "some," as he said, "tending to lasciviousness, and others to the detraction and scandal of some persons."

With no legal charges against Morton, Father said, Cap. Standish and his men seized him and put him in chains here in our village and returned him to England to be tried for who knows what. Father said the truth was the Separatists were scandalized by what they considered sinful behavior, particularly Englishmen consorting with Indian women. Moreover, Morton was of the Church of England and sold strong water and beer to the Indians and, worse, firearms. But, said Father, the truest reason for the persecution of Morton was the fact his colony, small as it was, had a better trade in beaver skins than we at Plymouth had.

25 April 1864, Eastham, Cape Cod

IN MORTON'S BOOK, which I think my ancestor never saw, for he never mentions it, Morton wittily calls Captain Standish "Captain Shrimp." The book is well worth reading, not only for the story of Merry Mount, but also for its thorough description of the flora and fauna of New England and its native inhabitants, whom Morton treated as equals, unlike the Separatists of Plymouth Colony (and, I may add, the Puritans of Massachusetts Bay Colony, of whom no less than Governor John Endicott was one; it was he, as Hawthorne tells us, who cut down the offending maypole and had "the lovelock and long glossy curls" of the newly-wed May Lord cut off, as the curls of Samson were shorn in the Old Testament. But this would have happened on the occasion of Morton's return to Merry Mount and has little to do with Giles's history). Nevertheless, I do not recommend the book to minors because of its lax morality. I would not want my nephews reading it until they reached the age of 21. If I become lax regarding this issue, Aunt Huldah's visits, now only once or twice a week, are sufficient to stiffen my resolve.

As Giles feels it necessary to record an episode that involved his father's two man servants, Edward Doty and Edward Lester, I will transcribe his story here. I leave, as usual, the spelling of the proper names intact.

c. 1623-24, New Plymouth, from the Memoir of Giles Hopkins

EDWARD DOTEY AND Edward Leister, Father's two indentured servants, were never close-knit in their friendship.

Indeed, as they had to be in the company of one another day after day, sleeping in the same house, eating together, etc., their friendship dwindled away like daub in our chimney.

If they were wont to patch their differences it was only because my Father encouraged them thus, not, I think, because of any disposition from their quarters. As for me, I was happy to have them, for they lessened my burden in the daily work we all of us had to do. Because they had identical Christian names, we were wont to call them by their surnames.

Be that as it may, Dotey and Leister became so contentious one afternoon over who would do the plowing and who repair a fence, they determined the only way to get satisfaction was to duel--the first in New England to do so-- with sword and dagger. Dotey got stabbed in his left hand, and Leister in his right thigh. Their punishment, decreed by Bradford and his council, was that they be bound head to feet for twenty-four hours without food or drink. Father so pled for them, as they for themselves, that after an hour of such punishment they were set free, promising never to repeat the offense.

Giles does not speculate as to why, apart from a general feeling of humanity, Stephen Hopkins should have been so kind to his servants, but my belief is that he recalled how in the Bermudas he himself was so shackled and condemned. Perhaps that experience accounts, as it does for so much else in his behavior, for his change in character.

CHAPTER FOUR
THE FURTHER HISTORY OF STEPHEN HOPKINS,
HIS SON, GILES, TOGETHER WITH THE HISTORIES
OF GABRIEL AND MARGARET WHELDEN,
THE DEATH OF HOBBAMOCK, THE HISTORIES OF
WABAN, ALSO CALLED NETOP,
CALEB HOPKINS, AND OTHERS

25 MAY 1864, EASTHAM, CAPE COD

HORRENDOUS NEWS! NATHANIEL Hawthorne has died, and in Plymouth, of all places, though not the Plymouth of my ancestors but of New Hampshire. I happened to be on one of my periodic trips to Boston to attend to my business. There I read in the newspaper that Hawthorne was on a carriage journey with his old friend, the former President, Franklin Pierce. He went to sleep and never woke up: the 19th of May 1864. And the war shows no sign of abatement. The slaughter continues. One more casualty. What shall I do? He will never read the story of Plymouth as told by Giles Hopkins. I must carry on, if only for the sake of my own peace of mind and for the benefit of my family. Perhaps the public at large will want to know Giles's story after this dreadful war is finished.

Therefore, I continue with my transcript. Here Giles discusses his wife, Catherine, and her family, the Wheldens, with a brief mention of my namesake, his half-brother, Caleb:

1623, THE WHELDENS IN PLYMOUTH COLONY, FROM THE MEMOIR OF GILES HOPKINS

ABOUT THE TIME my brother, Caleb, came into the world, so did my wife, Catherine. Needless to say, I had no knowledge of her birth at the time, nor indeed of her parents, whose history I shall now endeavour to convey so that the true history of my family will be set down for future generations.

My wife is the daughter of Gabriel Whelden and the daughter of Quadequina, the younger brother of Massasoit and a sachem himself. Gabriel and two of his brothers came from England on the *Charity,* the larger of the two ships that brought Thomas Weston's men. When things began to go so terribly wrong, as I have already written of, Gabriel and his brothers absconded to the west of Plymouth and found themselves in the territory of Massasoit and his brother, Quadequina. Being three Englishmen, they were conveyed by the Indians to Quadequina, who generously fed them as was their custom.

Gabriel beseeched Quadequina not to reveal who they were to Massasoit or any of the Englishmen for fear they would be charged with desertion and put in chains. As my father-in-law told me the story many years later, Quadequina sent his scouts to Plymouth to discover if what Gabriel and his brothers said about the Weston men were true. When his scouts returned with confirmation of the Englishmen's words, Quadequina agreed to allow them to stay with his people.

Like Thomas Morton, Gabriel, and to a lesser extent his brothers, admired the Indians and the admiration was mutual. Gabriel showed the warriors how to use muskets, and the warriors in turn showed them many things about how to make weapons for battle and for hunting and fishing. Among the weapons they learned to make were bows and arrows (which included arrow heads, shafts, and how to attach the feathers at the ends of the shafts), hatchet clubs, and ball-headed clubs. They would have preferred to use their pieces, but they had no way of recharging them after their gunpowder was used up.

It was not long before Gabriel's eyes turned to the beautiful youngest daughter of Quadequina. She was almost as tall as he was, with lovely, long black hair, and she was not as plump as many of the other maidens and mothers. One of his brothers, Ralph (after whom Gabriel later named one of his own sons), also came to love an Indian maiden among the villagers, and both of the brothers obtained permission to marry the maidens.

Massasoit, as ye may imagine, was not pleased to discover what had happened, for he feared the Plymouth governor and his council would be displeased, as indeed they were. Because his brother was the father of Gabriel's bride, whom he named Margaret after the wife he had in England (no one but his brothers knew about this until much later when word came she had died in England), Massasoit interceded with the Plymouth authorities, and an agreement was reached to the effect that the brothers and their brides would be banished from Plymouth and sent to live at Mattachees (which is called Yarmouth today). In lieu of the tribute owed him from the sachem at Mattachees, Massasoit asked that he take these people and allow them some land on which to build their houses and their farms. It was agreed. The third brother returned to England. None of this is recorded in the Plymouth Colony Court Records because the records dating before 1633 were destroyed, as ye know.

C. 1628, GILES AND WABAN, HIS WAMPANOAG FRIEND, FROM THE MEMOIR OF GILES HOPKINS

FORGIVE ME. MY chronicle threatens to waver. Let us return to my youth. I have always relied on my family and my friends. For sustenance, education, loyalty, and spiritual support, my family, and especially my father, have been my mainstays. My own particular humour has from my early days in London required the boon companionship of a friend. This office was fulfilled by Trevor Baker in Old England. In New England I had two, neither of which was wholly approved, I fear, by my father--or my mother--yet who can govern one's affection for, or indeed against, another? Perhaps the Separatists had found a way. I had not.

You have read the names of my two brave friends--John Cooke and Waban. Of Cooke, more later. Now I wish to write of Waban. As ye must have discerned by now, I had from childhood an affection, to use that word in both its positive and negative aspects, for the savage, a word used so often by the adults in my life, including my father, I found myself using it without thinking it might offend. Since the native peoples knew not our language, how could it offend?

But they are not barbarians, or, to be more precise, they are no more barbaric than are my English countrymen. Certainly, Hobbamock, our neighbor, was no savage, at least not after he had lived with us for some years. Frequently his own countrymen came to beseech him to live among them. By the customs of their people, he should be living with the family of his first wife. Although in general among the Pokanoket the men were the chiefs (there were exceptional women leaders whom we called "squaw sachems," often the wives of dead sachems), still the inheritance ran along the female lines. I know this from Waban and from my own wife, and from seeing and listening to Hobbamock's many visitors over the years. They did try to shame him by asking why he would prefer to behave like an Englishman, especially after what they had done to the Massachusetts at Wessagusett. They taunted him; they made fun of his new notions, such as putting a fence around his field of corn.

His answer was that the Englishmen never interfered with his traditional practices. He, at least in the early years, brought up his children in the old ways, and he had two wives. No Englishman forced him to change, although they did not pretend they approved. "The English need me, and it is *Manitou* that I help them." By this he meant he was doing what his god would have him to do.

"Tisquantum thought as ye do. Look what happened to him."

"*Coanau'mwem.* You speak truth. Squanto was a *pniese*, as I am. He let *Hobbamock,* my namesake, overcome his vision. He could not be killed by men's weapons so the great spirit, *Kiehtan*, sent a sickness to take him to the spirit land, to the house of *Cauta'ntouwit. Sowa'nakit au'waw.*"

"*Wunnau'mwaw ewo'*," said one of the warriors to the other. "What makes you think ye are so different from Tisquantum?"

"I follow my vision," said Hobbamock. "When I was a boy like my Waban here I saw a floating island made of wood come to Patuxet, when Tisquantum too was just a boy. The men with coats came and they settled on this part of the great island we all share. I knew when the English came they were these men in my vision, and my work is to help them."

The warriors agreed the English had been good allies against the Narragansetts, but they refused to say "*manito'wock.*" The white men were not gods, not to them.

THE TIME FOR Waban's initiation into manhood had come. I had no idea what this meant nor what it entailed. We English people had no such thing as an "initiation" into adulthood. At sixteen, I was now taking part in military exercises with the men, and I had long been helping with constructing houses, mending fences, farming, hunting, trapping, and fishing. I supposed I was a man, though I had no authority in the house. What was all this that Waban had to do to become a "man"?

For starters, he disappeared. It was the beginning of December and one day I went over to Hobbamock's *noosh wetu* and asked for Waban. His mother said he was gone to become a warrior.

"A warrior?" I asked. "Who will he fight?" I realized this was a foolish question since I myself participated in regular practice sessions learning to fight with musket and knife.

"All Pokanoket boys learn to become warriors. They must be able to defend our people," she said.

"Right. Forgive me my questions."

"Don't worry," she said. "He will be back before the time of corn planting."

Corn planting? That meant he would be gone perhaps four months, as indeed he was. He returned around the middle of April. I did not recognize him at first, for he his hair was no longer parted in the middle and braided. Now it was shaved on both sides and in the middle his hair stood up, held by some kind of grease or oil. From there to his nose was painted a red stripe. He told me he had acquired a new name. It was secret and hard to say, so he asked me to call him "Netop," meaning "friend," and that is what I called him from then on.

He told me he had been blindfolded and sent into the forest alone at night, with only his knife, hatchet, wooden quiver, and bow and arrows. There he had to survive all winter by his own wits and skill, living on what he could hunt and any vegetables such as tubers he could find.

"Was that not a hard task?"

"Yes, my friend. That is why I had to do it, to prove I could survive. It was a test of my manhood."

"Did ye go hungry then?"

"Sometimes. That is what drove me on. I made my own shelter, a small *wetu*, and I hunted deer, beaver, even a fox. He is a tricky one to kill--so smart, quick, hard to see. Here is his tail."

He showed me the bushy tail.

"I did not waste one part of any animal. That would dishonor his spirit."

"What about vegetables? How did ye find them?"

"I had watched my mother and father, my aunts and uncles, and I knew where to look. Once I found the winter house of a muskrat. He ran from me, but I took some, not all, of his lily roots. To thank him, I left him enough to see him through the season."

Then he told me when he returned to his village, that is, the village his mother came from, he was given the most bitter herbs and other poisonous plants to eat.

"They made me vomit," Netop said. "Yet I had to eat them again and again until something like black blood came out. Then I drank healing medicine to bring me back. As ye can see, I am fine. It will soon be *se'quan*, and I can live as a warrior and marry if I wish."

"I hope that is not soon," I said. "I don't want you to move away."

"Not soon," he said. "I have much to show you, if ye are interested."

"Of course I am interested!" I said.

"Then give me your hand," he said. I did so, and he extended his tongue completely out of this mouth and licked my hand from my fingertips to my wrist." This did seem a little lewd to me, yet I did not question my Netop.

"You are my *nee'mat*, my brother, and my *netop*, my friend."

"Right you are," I said. I shook his hand, taken aback ever so slightly, and then we hugged tightly as if we were one body.

C. 1629, NETOP'S STORIES, PLYMOUTH, FROM THE MEMOIR OF GILES HOPKINS

THEN BEGAN MY Wampanoag lessons with my Netop. "We are people of the dawn," he said. "Without our powwows *nippa'wus*, the sun, would not rise in the morning.

"This is the story my father, a great *pniese*, taught me and which I believe about how our people came into the world. Two maidens were enjoying themselves in the sea: a bountiful, deep blue, deeper than the blue of the sky it was. They frolicked together with great pleasure when the froth of the water entered their private parts and made them with child.

"In due time they gave birth, one to a son and one to a daughter. Then they passed away to the Southwest, from where they had come. This son and daughter were our first father and mother."

"Rather like our Adam and Eve."

"Yes. I think ye are right. We have many similar beliefs."

MY LITTLE BROTHER, Caleb, had been sitting nearby, unbeknownst to us. He laughed and said, "I like your story, Netop. Is it in the Bible?"

Netop smiled. "No, it is not in your English Bible. It is in the Bible we keep in our heads." He pointed a finger at his head.

Caleb, who was five or six years of age at the time, giggled again. Can I touch your head, Netop?"

Indulgent to children, as his parents had been to him and were to his brothers and sisters, Netop said, "Of course, if ye can reach it."

Caleb jumped, stretching out his arm, trying to touch Netop's head. It was out of reach.

"I can't touch it, Netop. Please let me."

"All right," he said with a smile and bent down.

Caleb moved his fingers over the shaved bristles of Netop's head. "That feels like a brush," Caleb said, laughing. "I like it. It feels good!"

Netop smiled while Caleb thought for a while. "Why isn't your story in the Bible?" he said.

Netop was very patient with him. "We have different traditions," he said. "Different ways."

"How can you remember the stories if they're not written down?" Father had been teaching Caleb how to read, and he was just beginning to read the Authorized Version of the Bible and the Book of Common Prayer.

Netop smiled and sat down as if to tell a story. We joined him. "Well, *nippa'poos*, my child, it is like this. We pass our stories on generation to generation. My father was told this story by his father, who was told it by his father, and so on back into unknown times. Understand?"

101

Caleb had a doubting look on his face. "Consider it this way," I said. "Do you know the story of how your father and mother and Constance and I and your little sister, Damaris, and your brother, Oceanus, came to this land?" Both Damaris and Oceanus had died of the fever, and I doubted Caleb could remember them well.

"Yes," said he. "You came on a big boat called . . . I can't remember."

"The *Mayflower*."

"The *Mayflower*. Now I remember!"

"You see, ye learned that by hearing it from me and from Mother and Father. You didn't read it, did ye?"

"No."

"That's how Netop's people remember their stories too. They tell them over and again."

"I understand!" said Caleb. He was a smart lad.

"Do ye want to hear more stories, Caleb?" Netop asked.

"Of course!"

"Then I will tell you some, but not now. Now you must go see what your mother wants." Netop's home with his parents, although it was close, was not in sight of our house. The trees had grown up around it, so that it was not visible. From where we lived, it had always been just a small thing, barely visible to the naked eye before the trees obscured it.

1630, FIRST HANGING IN PLYMOUTH, FROM THE MEMOIR OF GILES HOPKINS

DEATH, THEN AS now, was never a stranger to us. For John Billington, the younger (he who had gotten lost on Cape Cod), it was perhaps a mercy, for he did not live to see his father, John Billington, the elder, hanged in 1630 for murder, the first execution in the colony. Billington lay in wait and shot young John Newcomen, with whom he had argued. This murder was only the worst of many offenses by the Billington family. Following the advice of my father and mine own wits, I never became close friends with Francis or his brother, John.

By the time their father was hanged, it had been three years since the cattle were divided among the colonists. We were in the seventh lot, and included with us Hopkinses were the Palmers and the Billingtons. Dealing with the Billingtons was now a little easier with their querulous patriarch gone.

1630, NETOP'S STORIES CONTINUED, PLYMOUTH, FROM THE MEMOIR OF GILES HOPKINS

NETOP CONTINUED TELLING his people's stories to me and to my brother Caleb, always on Sabbath afternoon, between services, a time when by law we did not work. After that first day I wished Caleb would leave Netop and me alone and go play with children his own age. But Netop seemed to enjoy having him there, and sometimes other children would come. One of them was Mawpaw, Netop's half-brother, who was about the same age as Caleb. I did not wish to interfere.

Would to God I had interfered. Could I have seen what lay ahead, how my half-brother and Netop's half-brother would come to form an unnatural relationship, I would have stopped our Sabbath meetings then and there. May God forgive me for what ensued.

"NOW," NETOP SAID one Sunday afternoon. "Would you like to hear how corn came to us?"

Of course the answer was yes. So Netop told the story of Mon-do-min, a tribal hunter who was too old and crippled to hunt any longer: "One night he sat in his *wetu* by the side of a river, away from the other *wetus* in his village. He was cold and hungry, and the Wind Spirit was so unhappy that night he stirred up a storm.

"'Oh *Kiehtan*, Great Spirit,' said the old man, 'please help me. I am so hungry. Can you send me something from your heavenly home?'

"Soon he heard bird sounds from above. There was a partridge trapped in the top of his *wetu*. 'Oh thank you Great Spirit; you have brought me food so that I may not starve to death.' Mon-do-min lit a fire and began to fix the bird for his dinner.

"Not long after this, however, when the storm rested a bit, he heard the plaintive cries of a woman. She had got lost in the woods and had found respite from the storm under part of the Great Rock.

"With tremendous effort, the old man hobbled outside and brought in the suffering woman. He put her on his bearskin bed and rubbed her sore arms and legs, for she had tumbled in the mud and she shivered.

"'She must have something to eat!' he thought. So he took the little partridge from the fire and fed it to her, saying, 'This was given me by *Kiehtan*, but you must have it. There is only enough for you. Eat it and live. As for me, I shall die. It is the will of the Great Spirit. Do not forget me when you see others alone and dying. As I have done for you, do the same to them. Good-bye.'

"Mon-do-min lay down on the cold earthen floor, and during the night the Great Spirit carried him to his home in the Southwest, where all souls go after death. When the next

104

morning the woman found him there, she went to the village and told the sachem of the tribe. The people buried him on the river bank near his *wetu*.

"When spring arrived, at the place where Mon-do-min was buried green sprouts came up and spread over the area. They had green leaves wider than those of grass and better to behold. As they wondered what this could be on the grave of Mon-do-min, the Great Spirit said to them from above: 'Lo my children. When this you behold before ye be grown fully, it shall be ears of corn, food for you. Call it Mon-do-min after the one who took in the poor and dying one that raging night. When he himself was dying, he gave her to eat so that she might live. Remember this story and repeat it to your sons and daughters and to all your tribes when you see the green leaves sprouting.'"

There was silence for a moment. Then Caleb piped up: "But Father says we got the corn from the Indians."

"That is true," said Netop. "But we got it from the Great Spirit, as I have told you."

"Oh," he said.

DURING THESE SABBATH afternoon sessions, my brother Caleb and I learned much about Wampanoag beliefs. We learned they had many gods, which they called *manitos*. These included the chief god, the Great Spirit from the Southwest, *Kiehtan*, also called *Cauta'ntouwit*, the one who created, through the two sea women, human beings and brought them corn, or Mon-do-min. There was also the various spirit figures of Hobbamock, also called Cheepi. These came from the spirits of dead ones and could be seen in dreams and visions. From them the *pnieses* and powwows received their astounding powers. There were sun, moon, and star gods, gods for the directions, animals, wind, rain, snow, and so forth. And there was the giant hero, Maushop.

Netop's father was a *pniese* who had taken the name of his guiding spirit, *Hobbamock*, a powerful god who could hurt and even kill those who annoyed him. Only the young men with the most physical and spiritual strength became *pnieses*, for their initiations were even harsher than that Waban/Netop experienced. Netop's father had gone through the same ordeal of eating the bitter herbs; then he had to fast and then drink potions that gave him the ability to endure self-flogging and running the gauntlet through brambles, shrubs, and boles. *Hobbamock* had appeared to Netop's father in a vision during his initiation ritual. This meant the god had chosen him to be a special warrior and counselor to his sachem. He was to protect and serve the sachem by calling on *Hobbamock* in times of need. Always *pnieses* were respected for their bravery and moral judgment. Hobbamock was Massasoit's special emissary to us, the people of Plymouth, formerly Patuxet. And, while our Separatist leaders believed and preached that God had prepared the land for them by means of the epidemic that slew all the native inhabitants, the sachem of Pokanoket believed the English were there as allies against his enemies, the Narragansets. Still, through Hobbamock, he felt it important to keep an eye on his allies. This Netop only suggested. I'm not sure Caleb understood his meaning, but I certainly did.

NETOP TOLD US that the powwows had the power to swim under the water like a fish and soar through the air like an eagle. He also told of an enormous eagle that picked up children in his claws. The parents of the children followed

106

them to the island of Nantucket, where they found the bones of their children. At the end of this story Caleb, Mawpaw, and one or two of the other younger children began to cry.

"Do not cry, little ones," said Netop. "The story is meant to show the special *manitos* or spiritual power of the eagle, who comes from the sky and teaches us many things, such as loyalty, honor, and connection to the Great Spirit *Kiehtan*. We must always respect him and never let his feathers touch the ground. When that happens a ceremony of cleansing must be performed directly. If we honor the eagle, he will not harm us. He might even help us when we need him."

Another time Netop told us about a great white whale that existed before the Europeans came. The whale lived in a place called Witch Pond and would on occasion rise from the water. An ancient sachem, powerful and full of wisdom, had first told the story. He said it betokened the coming of men and women of a color like that of the whale, and the sachem warned his people not to give their land to the newcomers or they would be demolished as a people.

Caleb blurted out. "Is that story about me and Giles?"

"No, Caleb," said Netop. "It's not about you two. It is about your people."

"But I wouldn't take your land!"

"I know," said Netop. "But some of your people might and, indeed, have done so already."

"Not me!"

"I know," said Netop, patiently.

This seemed to satisfy Caleb. I looked for any signs of enmity in Netop's eyes. I found none.

WHEN A PERSON needed healing whether from disease or an injury in battle, powwows, Netop said, had the power to take onto themselves the sickness or the wound of the ailing person. They could become an eagle or a Thunderbird, leave this material world and cross over to the spirit world. If they did not do this through the air, they could become the horned water serpent and renew the life of the sick person, restore balance: that was the goal, the purpose in healing, to reach the center, one of the seven directions, the others being up, down, north, south, east, and west. The world tree, as seen etched into rock or on amulets, like these other spirit figures, represented the balance of all directions. The English had little or no sense of the powwow powers and symbols, nor, with few exceptions, did they care. To them all Indian religion was devil worship.

DURING THE COURSE of one of these Sabbath sessions, Netop happened to mention a "squaw sachem."

"What's a 'squaw sachem'?" Caleb asked.

"She is sort of like your Queen Elizabeth I have heard of," said Netop. When there is no suitable man to become sachem, we choose a woman. Sometimes she is the widow of the old sachem or she could be his sister or daughter.

"Let me tell you a story about a warrior woman, the daughter of a sachem named Hiwassee. From the Island of Nope, she was the most beautiful maiden ever seen there. Taller than the other maidens, her long black hair was shiny like the raven's, and even though she was as graceful as a maiden should be, she greatly surpassed all the other women in the abilities that usually belong to a man. She was the best with bow and arrows, the best torturer of prisoners, the best war-dancer, and the best singer of war songs.

"According to our tradition, she taught the women to wear the claw of the crab in their noses and the clam shell in their lower lips for ornamentation. Many men came to her *wetu* to try to win her with gifts of conch-shells, eagle feathers, and much wampum. But her love had long belonged to a handsome young warrior on the other side of the island, the son of a devil, some said.

"However, parents do not always approve of their children's choices in love. The father of this beautiful warrior woman told her the young warrior she loved had killed only three enemies and was not descended from sachems.

"What could the lovers do but seek help from the giant, Maushop. Now Maushop had resolved to annoy all young lovers, but fortunately for this young pair, his mood was altered by two happenings. One, a number of whales had beached themselves near the opening of his cave, providing delicious food. And two, Maushop's brother goblin, who lived on the mainland, had supplied him with some fine vintage tobacco.

"All this put old Maushop in the mood to assist the warrior maiden and her lover. He went immediately to Hiwassee to inquire what his objections to the union of the two lovers were. Not wasting any words, the sachem said: 'He is not famous, he is poor, and he comes from a common line.'

"'And what would make you change your mind, Hiwassee?'

"'If the young man had his own island--that would change my mind.'

"Maushop inhaled deeply from his pipe and said, 'Good. Come with me.'

109

"Maushop led the sachem and the others to the other side of the island. There he commenced his incantations, blowing much smoke, digging in the earth, placing hot stones in the hole, chanting, bowing to the dawn sun and the North Star, blowing three times from a conch-shell, and smoking so much that it became very dark. Then he emptied his pipe. Red-hot embers fell into the sea water. The west wind blew the smoke over the water and, lo and behold, an island emerged from it, created by the ashes Maushop had emptied from his pipe. Maushop gave the couple the island, and they called it Nantucket, and so it is called today."

Caleb, as was his wont, had need to know more. "Where is Nantucket?" he asked.

Netop was never impatient with Caleb's questions, or indeed with the questions any of the children would ask. "It's an island, as ye now know, south of here. Maybe someday we can go there."

Caleb thought the idea a joyous one, and he asked if we would go in Netop's canoe, which we had watched him build from a large pine log he had cut in the forest. He took many, many days to burn out a hollow in the log and then make the hollow smooth with the shells of clams and oysters.

"Of course we can go in my canoe," said Netop.

MAUSHOP WAS HIMSELF turned into a great white whale, said Netop another time, for cosseting too much the people. One of the Wampanoag whalers killed him. Netop believed only a Wampanoag could kill a creature so coveted by those who hunt whales. His friend, the toad, was so distraught at the loss of Maushop, the Great Spirit turned him into stone which looked like a frog as a lesson never to grieve

110

too much over what our Creator has decided. His decisions are always best for all creatures.

Here I must tell you, my dear family, that I had no idea my little half-sister, Ruth, was hidden away, secretly listening to Netop's stories. This woman-warrior story must have deeply impressed her, for later she fell into her own unnatural relationship. And, I may add, I myself was tempted into such a sinful direction. By the grace of God, I resisted, unlike my brother, Caleb, and my sister, Ruth. I will tell you what happened in due time.

C. 1636, A TRIP TO A WAMPANOAG VILLAGE, FROM THE MEMOIR OF GILES HOPKINS

WE NEVER WENT to Nantucket with Netop, but he did invite us to join in a harvest celebration at the village of his mother. Our mother was apprehensive about our going, for Caleb was only twelve or thirteen years of age. Father assured her we would be all right, particularly as I was going. He trusted Hobbamock and Netop as well.

Caleb and I, together with Hobbamock, his two wives, Netop, and all the children, walked single-file through the forest. I never ceased to marvel at the Indian trails which led through the trees. They are well-worn paths that an Englishman could easily miss they are so well hidden among amidst the foliage of the forest.

The village was a day and a half's journey, so we slept overnight by a fire, eating the parched corn the hunters and warriors generally carry with them in their leather pouches. Netop killed a rabbit, and the second of Hobbamock's wives roasted it over the fire. Although Hobbamock and Netop had tobacco pouches hanging from their necks down their backs, no one smoked that night. Perhaps they were saving the tobacco for the celebrations.

On our journey, we passed several "memory holes," as Netop called them. These were places where certain important events had occurred. To remember them, the holes were made. One of these had been filled by soil and leaves. Netop cleared these out and told us the story of what had happened here. A certain village had been suffering from a drought at this place. Their powwow led the people in a great rain dance, and within a day rain came and saved the people.

When we arrived at the village, there were already perhaps two hundred or more people gathered and another village of two hundred came to join in the festivities. I saw men in circles playing a game called *puim,* with stalks of grass, which they shuffled like cards (the playing of which the leaders of Plymouth did not countenance) and distributed amongst the players. We had heard the noise from their shouting long before we saw the village.

Other men were playing a game called *hubbub*, in which they tossed five small bits of bones painted white on one side and black on the other, much like dice. The tossing is done on a tray, and the player wins the round if three pieces are of the same color. When a man loses, he must surrender the tray and pass it to another.

During our three or four days at the festivities, I saw a number of men who were playing when we went to sleep still playing in the morning. Netop said they had not stopped to eat, drink, or sleep, and never an argument amongst them, even when a man had lost everything he had--his wampum, his clothing, his bow and arrows, his tomahawk, his tobacco

112

pouch, even his breech cloth. Some have even gambled their lives, said Netop, but I never saw that myself.

The men also played a game similar to our English football, along a path by the river nearly a mile long. The players paint themselves as if they were preparing for war, but this is to prevent recognition of any from the other village who might accidentally hurt another and thus begin a fight, which would be against the customs of the sport. The ball is so small it can be encircled by a hand and the goal is a long distance away, from one end of the path to the other. The ball can be moved forward with the feet, either by one man or by a group of men. It may take two days to win the goal.

Before the sport starts, the players, all men, hang their weapons in a tree and lovingly shake hands and then they begin the rough struggle to win, all this while the boys and the women are dancing and singing. Among the players was one who had the appearance of a man but who had, if my eyes did not lie, female breasts. I meant to ask Netop about this person, but he was playing in a game of *puim*, and I did not want to disturb him. Pondering now the fate of my sister, Ruth, I wish could have warned her. But I am no prophet or seer.

The football game is followed by a feast for all the players, and I observed this woman-man did not follow the customs of the women but that of the men. She did not prepare the food; she consumed it with the other players. Was she like the warrior woman of Netop's tale?

"Yes," said Netop when I seized an opportunity to question him. "This is Pequas, meaning a 'fox.' (The fox is a clever yet beautiful trickster among the Indians.) She is the daughter of Tantum, our village sachem, and she is the one who gave me my secret name. Please not to tell your father or the other English at Plymouth. They would try to kill Pequas, I believe."

Mystified as I was, I did not wish to betray my friend or his people, and I agreed the Separatists would find some law to justify hanging Pequas. I promised to say nothing and have not done so till now, when all danger to Pequas is passed.

FOOTBALL WAS NOT the only sporting game. They also had contests of shooting their bows and arrows, footracing, and swimming, for they are powerful swimmers. The winners receive wampum, Indian gold, the brown skins of beavers and the black skins of otters.

Every evening we feasted on venison, wild turkey, waterfowl, many dishes of corn, beans, squash, fishes, etc. No one went hungry, as is the custom with all the Indians the year round. The poor are taken care of. Moreover, in the games, the sachem of the village and the powwows and *pnieses* all took part in the sporting and the games, some winning and some losing.

On the last day, they built a long house with more fires than I could count because of the many people who crowded into the place. Despite these many people, numbers of them danced and then those who had the means gave away their skins, knives, wampum, and anything else they might have to the poor, who would bid them do so. It is considered a grave disgrace not to give freely.

The dances are a spectacle unknown to English eyes. They are not disorganized as they might seem to a stranger to Indian customs. Each dancer, be he man, woman, or child, follows particular patterns with the feet and arms, whilst others sing and beat the ground with their feet in amazing rhythms that defy those we are accustomed to. They whoop in such loud yelps those of our Separatists who have heard them, and even others who are not bound by that sect, have claimed they are worshipping the devil. This I believe is nonsense, for although they believe in mischief-making spirits, they do worship in their own ways a god (or gods) that come from traditions much practiced for generations.

My brother Caleb had before we left become painted like the other boys of his age and was dancing and singing and swimming and such like as if he were an Indian himself. I resolved not to tell our parents about this for fear they would spoil his joy and forbid his visiting the house of Hobbamock.

5 JULY 1864, EASTHAM, CAPE COD

WHAT IS ALL this about? Unnatural relationships, a warrior woman, a woman-man—what on earth was going on among my ancestors? Did Aunt Huldah know about such goings on, and is this knowledge behind her ghostly admonitions, which lately have dwindled to one or two a month? I suspect I shall soon find out.

AGAIN THERE SEEMS to be a gap in the manuscript of my ancestor. There are so many pages left for me to transcribe, and there are other papers I have yet to read. Here I think I shall insert copies of two letters from Gabriel Whelden to his brother, Ralph, who returned to England. Gabriel must have got someone else to write his letters, for he himself could read and write only a little.

3 JANUARY 1639, YARMOUTH, LETTER FROM GABRIEL WHELDEN TO HIS BROTHER, RALPH

MY DEAR BROTHER Ralph,

I know how awfully sad your homecoming to Nottinghamshire must have been without your dear, lamented late wife. Such knowledge makes me all the more thankful that you should return to our home country to oversee our property, such as it is.

After living so long with my dear wife, Margaret, amongst the inhabitants of Mattacheese, amongst, that is, her people (or a tribe belonging to her people), I have desired to make provision for my children's future and therefore become a lawful member of the English community that is beginning to settle in these parts. To that end I became, along with Gregory Armstrong, a joint-tenant of the house and property of Mr. Stephen Hopkins of Plymouth. Mr. Armstrong, being without a wife, lives with my family.

The council at Plymouth will not grant Mr. Hopkins leave to live here, so for the moment he has hired us to keep his cattle. I see great possibilities for the future and have already applied for permission to own my land, which I and Margaret have been cultivating these many years.

This permission, I am glad to tell ye, has been granted, and the son of Mr. Hopkins, Giles, has been pleased to share the company of my daughter, Katherine. I think our two families may very well be united and that the disgrace of my marriage to a savage, as they would call her, will be assuaged at last.

The name of this place is now called Yarmouth by the council of Plymouth.

Your loving brother,
Gabriel

Yarmouth, 3rd January 1639

10 OCTOBER 1639, YARMOUTH, LETTER FROM GABRIEL WHELDEN TO HIS BROTHER, RALPH

MY DEAR BROTHER Ralph,

I am very pleased to confirm that the prophesy of my last letter has been fulfilled. Giles Hopkins did marry my first-born child, Catherine, on the 9th of October 1639, in Plymouth.

With this marriage my family is now incorporated back into the good graces of our countrymen, albeit I and my wife are not allowed still to live in New Plymouth. This is of no matter. She and I do not wish to live under the piercing eyes of the strictly religious people there. In fact, my new son-in-law has the same opinions, for he has long been under suspicion because of his unprejudiced contacts with the Indians, and indeed I may say that this humour in him opened him to the possibilities of wedded happiness with my dear Catherine.

He and Catherine are going to live in the house his father built and in which my family and Gregory Armstrong have been living. Gregory and I will for now continue to help tend the cattle which belongs primarily to Stephen Hopkins, but I and my family will be cultivating our own property, as before. We shall return to our old house as well.

I am glad to hear you are prospering. In the future, not soon, we must consider selling our property. But do not bother about that now.

Your loving brother,
Gabriel
Yarmouth, 10th October 1639

5 July 1864, Eastham, Cape Cod

THIS IS QUITE interesting. Pieces of the mystery of my ancestors are starting to fit together. Perhaps, dear reader, you are wondering what happened to some of the other persons in Giles's narrative. The answers should come in the following pages of his manuscript as I transcribe them. We shall see.

1633-36, Stephen Hopkins and Plymouth, from the Memoir of Giles Hopkins

MANY THINGS HAPPENED during those few years when my brother Caleb was growing past childhood and our Sabbath sessions came to an end. There were always murmurs of complaint about the sessions. John Cooke sat in on one or two of them and reported what happened to his father, Francis. This action on his part changed my opinion of him. After that I spoke to him as a fellow villager, not as a friend. Francis must have repeated what his son said to my father, who had been selected as one of the assistants to the governor of Plymouth: first to Edward Winslow, then to Mr. Thomas Prence, and then again to William Bradford. Instead of stopping our conversing with Netop and his family, as might have been the expected result, we were allowed to continue, as long as we did attend Sabbath services and did not spread "devilish" ideas from the savages, as our friends were called. I think my father, being in a position of influence, persuaded the governor and the other members of the governor's council that no harm would be done by our being friends with the Indians and, in fact, that perhaps some good would be the result of our friendly relations if only we would tell them about the Gospel.

1636-37, CALEB HOPKINS'S ILLNESS AND THE DEATH OF HOBBAMOCK, FROM THE MEMOIR OF GILES HOPKINS

TWO EVENTS OCCURRED that put an end to our Sabbath sessions. Caleb became so sick it seemed he would die. Our own physician, Samuel Fuller, had died during a season of infectious fever in which several others had died, and we had no physician to succeed him. Edward Winslow came to try his healing powers, which had worked so well on Massasoit. But he was of no help to my brother.

Netop had never told us that he had had a vision and become a powwow. Unlike the Separatists, he never attempted to make us come over to his religion, and I suppose that is why he kept quiet about his new position among his people. When I told Netop about Caleb's illness, he asked if my father and mother would be open to his coming to do what he could to heal Caleb. I told him to wait just a while until I could talk to my father.

When it was clear Winslow and none of the others who offered medicinal herbs and remedies were helping, my father asked me to bring Netop. "Would that God take not another of my children!" my father said.

Netop said he would do what he could, but we must clear the house of all but me and Caleb and a helper from Pokanoket, none other than Pequas, the woman-man I had seen at the harvest celebrations. Father agreed, but I am sure he waited outside the door all the time till Netop was finished with his work.

Even to this day, so late in my life, I find telling what happened in our house so difficult I can hardly breathe as I write. When Netop and his helper arrived, they both wore painted faces, black, red, and white, and wampum around their necks, arms, and legs. I saw a change in Netop's eyes, as if he had been transported to another world. He spoke as a natural person, as the Netop I knew as my friend, but when we came inside the house, he and Pequas lit some freshly dried tobacco and waved it in the air. Then they began chanting as I had heard Indians chant in the few times Netop took me to their ceremonies, yet this was keener in both pitch and intensity, and the wampum jingled like bells as they beat their chests, making loud, lamentable noises and prayers. I recognized only a few words, words such as *"Kiehtan"* and *"Hobbamock"* and *"Cheepi."* Surely Netop and Pequas weren't calling on evil spirits. Netop had brought a potion, and he put it to Caleb's lips. Caleb sipped, then coughed so hard he shook.

The ritual went on for about an hour; then they rested and did it again; and then they did it again and again till my friend was in a kind of stupor or trace. I was afraid and wanted to run from the house. Netop was not in the same world I was in. He waved eagle feathers over Caleb during each of these cycles and Pequas waved the skin of a snake, both murmuring words I could not comprehend but for *wobsacuck*, which means "eagle," and *askooke*, which means "snake." And then Netop put a crystal rock on Caleb's chest. Caleb jerked, as if it were a hot ember. And to me it looked as if the crystal radiated beams of light. Surely my mind was disarranged.

Netop put his lips to the lips of Caleb and made a great sucking sound. Then he gently climbed on the bed, his hands and feet like legs of a table over him, and, as Pequas chanted, walking back and forth around the bed, Netop sucked again and fell backwards and to the left side of the bed, without touching Caleb, and lay on the floor as if he were dead. There was a long silence; then I looked for help to Pequas, who was also in a trance. I could do nothing.

Of course we had prayed over Caleb from the beginning of his sickness. Now I thought to pray again, asking for God's mercy on my poor brother, asking Him to spare him too for our parents' sake.

After I know not how long time passed, I heard the door open and in walked my father, his head bowed like a dog that had been punished. "Is he all right?" he whispered.

"I do not know."

Father looked at Caleb, still lying there, breathing hard. He looked at Netop lying on the floor and at Pequas, sitting in a trace. Then he looked helplessly at me as if to say, "What shall we do?"

At that moment we heard a stir from the bed. Caleb's eyes were open, and he was resting on his elbows. "What happened?" he asked.

"Oh son," said Father, "Are ye all right? Are you better?"

He took a deep breath and said faintly, "Yes, I feel fine. May I have something to eat?"

Heaving a huge sigh, Father said, motioning to me, "Yes, of course you may eat."

I went to the pot over the fire, but nothing was there. So I went outside and found Mother standing fearfully by the door. She went to our nearest neighbor and brought back a bowl of pottage.

While Caleb was taking the food in small amounts, Netop arose from the floor. He shook himself slightly and asked, "How is Caleb?"

"I think he's over the worst of it," I said. "Thanks to you . . . and your friend." I saw Pequas had also returned to this world.

Father was so grateful he offered a musket to each of the healers, not knowing that Pequas was by birth a woman. Such gifts were forbidden by law, but Father was never one to bother much with laws. He knew that by custom, gifts were expected for any favors from the Indians. It was not the value of the gifts that mattered but the friendship they signified. He also gave them each a jar of strong water and some wampum,--all gladly accepted, as was the custom.

And that is the story of Caleb's healing by our friend and his strange helper. Netop had become, unknown to us, a powerful powwow of his own people. At that moment, we were the beneficiaries, but Father cautioned us not to tell those outside the family what had occurred. We could be banished if they knew the full truth.

In light of subsequent events, I wish my little sister, Ruth, had not known of these strange happenings and had not seen the face of the mysterious Pequas.

I am certain the whole village knew or guessed something unusual had happened in our house. How could they not? Everyone could hear the powwow noises. Only Father's position as the governor's assistant and his own history with the Indians kept him out of court. Yet I believe Caleb's illness and recovery marked the beginning of the end of our already intermittent Sunday sessions.

IT HAS OCCURRED to me that you, my children and my children's children, and any others who may chance to read my words, do not know what your Uncle Caleb looked like. He was an exceptionally beautiful boy, like the ancient stories that tell of Ganymede and Antinous, with olive skin close in colour to the skin of the Indians. His eyes were black, like those of Netop, and his black hair curly. His skin was so smooth and so clear no blemish seemed to have touched it, even after his serious illness. He was naturally muscular, and close in height to Netop, taller than most of his English fellows. If a comely appearance ran in our family, Caleb was the prime example of that trait.

Not long after Caleb had recuperated, Netop invited him and me to go with him and two of his younger brothers to a hothouse near the river by the village of his mother. Sweating in the house or lodge could heal the body and the spirit, said Netop. Even the French disease, if one takes certain medicines, can be healed by such means.

The hothouse was built with stones and rushes to cover it. It was just high enough for a man to stand in the middle. On the ground in the middle the Indians heated stones with a wood fire until the heat was almost unbearable.

We had to strip our clothes from our bodies and sit around the fire naked as water from a clay pot and an English bucket was poured onto the hot stones and steam rose so much that it was like a fog so thick ye could not see the person next to you. Sweat came from every part of our bodies, and a tobacco pipe with the effigy of a wolf or a lion on its end was passed around and we smoked whilst the Indians talked or sang.

I noticed that Netop called Caleb over to him, probably to monitor his strength or minister to his health, for he rubbed his hands on Caleb's neck, shoulders, arms, and legs. This I saw only briefly before the mist obscured them altogether. Because of the conversation and singing, I could not hear anything Netop and Caleb may have said to each other. On the other side of Caleb was Mawpaw, Netop's half-brother, who had become a handsome young man with his half-brother's good looks. Although he had a new Indian name after his initiation into manhood, he allowed us to call him Mawpaw as we were wont to do. He said it meant, "It snows," and if a person dreamt that it snowed the dream foretold good fortune for that person. After I know not how long, perhaps an hour, we left the lodge and ran into the cooling waters of the river. It was indeed refreshing to body and spirit.

THE SECOND EVENT the result of which put an end to the Sabbath sessions occurred shortly after this. More than once Caleb went into the forest with Netop, either alone or with Mawpaw. In general, most of the Indians were handsome compared to the Europeans. I was too busy with my adult affairs to accompany my brother on these adventures, which I was told consisted of hunting and fishing, together with swimming, running, and other sportive activities. As long as Caleb did his chores, Mother and Father did not scruple about his going with Netop and Mawpaw. Would that they had.

But to the second event. Hobbamock died. It happened quite suddenly. He had just come back from checking his traps when he fell ill. Netop was gone on one of his expeditions with Caleb and Mawpaw. Winslow was called in, as was my Father and me. Bradford came too. Hobbamock, against whom the laws of Plymouth were never enforced due to his innumerable and indispensable services to the colony, nevertheless had been attending church and on his deathbed asked, not unlike Squanto, that we Englishmen pray that he would enter our Heaven when he passed from this world. He also asked that we, my Father and I, look after his children and his wives. We of course promised we would. By the next morning his soul had left his body.

The lamentations which now began are such that ye have never heard. Our English women weep quietly and cry out but little when a loved one dies. Hobbamock's wives and children wailed as if they had been harpies from hell. Bradford and Winslow went to calm them, but Father held them back, saying, "Let them be. It is their way." I heard Winslow mutter: "They are like the Irish in their howlings."

I dreaded the moment when Netop, Mawpaw, and Caleb would return. That moment came around noon. Word had somehow come to them of the terrible happening, for they were running as they came. Netop and Mawpaw entered the house, and soon I heard their howlings added to those of the others in the *wetu*. Caleb asked Father if he should join them. Father said, "Let them be alone with their grief. You can comfort them when they are ready."

"We must prepare for a service," said Bradford, who had recently been selected to serve again as governor.

My father, serving still as assistant to the governor, said, "Let us wait and see what his family would prefer. We know his soul is at rest now. What does it matter if they wish to bury him according to their own manner?"

"The manners of heathen?" said Bradford, his face ugly with doubt and hatred.

"We do not want to stir up any trouble now."

Father was referring to the problems with the Pequot Indians, who were charged with the murders of John Stone and John Oldham, both traders who, as history has proved, were killed by other Indians, not the Pequots.

"Perhaps you are right," the governor said.

Netop and Mawpaw did not emerge from the *wetu* till evening. Their faces, and those of the rest of their family, were made black with the ashes from the fire.

Netop spoke for the family: "Tomorrow we will take my father to the village of his mother so we may bury him as is proper so his spirit may be with *Kiehtan*."

Nobody would dare dispute Netop's word. He told me later that he and his people believe the spirit of a dead person who has led a good life goes to the spirit world in the Southwest. Their heaven is like this world in the late spring. The gardens bloom with sweet-scented flowers, the corn is abundant, the meadows a rich green; they take sweat baths as they wish and swim in temperate streams and rivers, enjoying sensual pleasure untainted by any questions of fidelity or mischief. Their dwellings protect them perfectly from any tempests, and they know neither pain nor sorrow. Nature provides everything they need.

At the gate to this paradise lies a gigantic dog, rather like a one-headed Cerberus, refusing entrance to the unworthy--the ungenerous, liars, and cheaters--and to their enemies. These go to the hell of *Hobbamock,* the spirit, were they are tortured like prisoners of war. It sounded very much like the hell we heard of from the pulpit.

Father, Caleb, and I were the only representatives from our village allowed to follow Hobbamock's funeral party to his burial place. Netop refused permission to anyone else, remembering the treatment they had inflicted on the Massachusett Indians of Wessagusett. Referring to Bradford, Winslow, and Standish, Netop said, "They would defile the very ground in which my father will lie." I could not dispute the fact.

Even though he had lived away for so long and they had seen him but little since the time we colonists arrived, Hobbamock's village responded as if he had been their sachem, living with them daily. All wore black faces and loudly lamented their and the family's loss as if it were their own. "*Sachimaûpan*," they said, meaning "He was a prince here," for they did not like to say the name of the dead. The scorn they held for those who would say the name of the dead was so great the penalty could range from a mere reprimand to a fine to even a war if the name were that of an important sachem and was used by their enemies. Since *Hobbamock* is also the name of a spirit, the context was everything. If one spoke of the spirit, that was condoned; if one spoke of the man, that was condemned.

After a day or two of lamentations, the sachem of the village and the chief powwow and *pnieses* attempted to comfort the family. They said, "*Kutchímmoke, Kutchímmoke,*" meaning, "Be of good cheer." As they said these soothing words, they caressed the faces and heads of Hobbamock's wives and his children.

Now came a surprise to us all, for Pequas came. Her face was also painted black, and they addressed her as "*Mockuttásuit,*" meaning one of the highest regard whose task it is to dig the burial hole, wrap the dead in his shroud, and bury him. I doubt not that Father thought her a man. To the others she was a person of wisdom, honored as a powwow and *pniese,* chosen by the family for her task.

After she was greeted, Pequas was taken to the deceased. She wailed with the others for a long time. Then they took her into the great *wetu* of the sachem of the village and she feasted.

127

The next day Massasoit himself came with a hundred or more of his warriors. Minor sachems came too with their men. Pequas dug the grave outside the limits of the village as the family, the sachems, and all the others in order of their positions in Wampanoag society sat and mourned, tears making lines in the black paint they wore.

When the digging was done, Pequas gently wrapped Hobbamock in an English blanket. I suppose this was done in honor of his life work as an emissary to the English. With the help of Netop, Mawpaw, and the village sachem, they lay the body in a fetal position, facing the Southwest, on the mat upon which he died. He was leaving this world, I was told, as he came into it, facing the direction of the house of *Kiehtan*, where he was going. To help him on his journey, they buried with him his bow and arrows, his tomahawk, his spear, and plenty of victuals in case he got hungry. They put one of his deer skin garments on a nearby tree to let it decay as the body would decay. On the body they placed the best of his garments and wampum and over him another mat. Then Pequas covered the body with the dirt from the hole she had dug.

After this was done, they again made such a noise of mourning I felt as if I were in hell myself, yet all three of us, my father, my brother Caleb, and I, wept as if for our own flesh and blood. Indeed, I could not help but recall the passings of my mother and my sisters, Elizabeth (the first), Damaris (the first), and my brother, Oceanus. I admit that thoughts of my old friend, Trevor, came to me as I wondered whether he be alive or not at this moment.

According to their traditions, Hobbamock's house must be destroyed, and no one was to talk of him again. The mourning period was to last nearly a year, and during that

time there was no more playing of games, nor decorating
their bodies for comeliness, nor could they get into quarrels
or violence with any other. To do any of these things would
have been dishonour to the dead.

ALL OF THIS meant that Netop and his family were no
longer our neighbors. Neither I nor Caleb could play
sportive games, hunt, or fish with Netop, Mawpaw or any of
their family. The Sabbath sessions, it need not be said,
stopped, as did all story telling by Netop. The death of
Hobbamock also spared me and Caleb any possible
disagreement or embarrassment over our military activities,
for we both, along with our father, volunteered to fight the
Pequots along with our neighbor colonies, the Massachusetts
Bay Colony and Connecticut. The Pequots, in any event,
were enemies of Netop and his people.

CHAPTER FIVE
THE PEQUOT WAR,
THE FURTHER HISTORIES OF
STEPHEN, GILES, AND CALEB HOPKINS,
VARIOUS CRIMES OF THE FLESH,
&
THE MARRIAGE OF GILES AND CATHERINE,
ETC.

19 JULY 1864, EASTHAM, CAPE COD (THE PEQUOT WAR, 1637; THE UNITED STATES GOVERNMENT AND THE INDIANS IN 1864)

HERE THERE IS another gap in the manuscript by my ancestor, Giles Hopkins. This time information is missing. There is a tear apparently caused by a fire at the end of one piece of parchment and a simple tear, probably caused deliberately by hand in another. Giles says almost nothing about what help, if any, he and his father gave to Hobbamock's family. He also says almost nothing else about the Pequot War, so I have been obliged to discover through what sources I could find what happened during that war and whether my ancestors changed course and actually perpetrated violence on the Indians they seem so to have admired, albeit the English made war not on the Wampanoag tribe but on a neighboring one.

Like many of the wars our federal government has instigated against the native inhabitants of this continent, the Pequot War seems to have been perpetrated by well-known causes: to further the power of the government (in this case the New England colonies of Massachusetts Bay and Connecticut, and, indeed, of Plymouth) over the native inhabitants, to enforce the conversion of those natives to the religion of the colonists (I need not add that the religion was Puritanical Christianity), and to acquire land for the growing numbers of settlers coming from England at this time. This last motivation, I have no doubt, was the primary reason for the Pequot War. So far as I can tell, nobody tried to convert the Pequots to Christianity before they were slaughtered.

One need search no further than the periodicals of our day to find contemporary examples of the government's abuse of our aboriginal peoples. I read in the papers that the federal government, now engaged, as our President Lincoln says, "in a great civil war," has chosen to spare men who could have been used in that war to instead subdue the Mescalero Apaches in the territory of New Mexico and incarcerate them in something called the "Bosque Redondo Reservation," where, in this very year (1864) they have, with the aid of Colonel Kit Carson imprisoned thousands of the Apaches' traditional enemies, the Navajo, in the same place after having burned their hogans and destroyed their cultivated fields in eastern Arizona and western New Mexico and having forced them to walk hundreds of miles through a treacherous desert to their place of incarceration.

As if fighting and imprisoning the Apaches and the Navajo were not enough, during the period of this same civil war (and the decades before it) the government has also made war against the Santees in Minnesota, the Tetons in North Dakota, and the Sioux in North Dakota and South Dakota. By this very year, 1864, Generals Henry Hastings Sibley and Alfred Sully have slaughtered, I read, some 90 per cent of the Santee and hundreds of the Teton who had tried to protect them when they fled from Minnesota to North Dakota. The price on Sioux scalps has reached $200 in Yankton, South Dakota, where Gen. Sully, in the manner of Captain Standish in Plymouth, placed two Teton heads on poles for all to see.

It would appear to me, though I am no military expert nor even a proponent of war, that Colonel Kit Carson, Generals Sibley and Sully and their men could better use their military expertise to win that civil war Mr. Lincoln says is being fought to save that nation "conceived in liberty, and dedicated to the proposition that 'all men are created equal.'" I wonder, does that include those enslaved Negroes in the southern states? Apparently it does, for Mr. Lincoln last year declared them free in his Emancipation Proclamation. Does the phrase, "all men are created equal," apply also to the Indians?

Excuse me, dear reader, I have digressed again. I was about to tell you what I have learned regarding the Pequot War, which was, in fact, the first of our colonial wars against the Indians.

Although the grounds for the enmity against the Pequot tribe were based on their supposed killing of the traders, John Stone and John Oldham, as Giles has written, the Pequots were not responsible for these murders. While a Massachusetts Bay military party under John Endicott searched for the purported murderers of Stone and Oldham, Cutshamekin, a Massachusett sachem, slew a Pequot and sent his scalp to the great Narragansett sachem, Canonicus, thus sealing by this symbol the ties between the Massachusetts and the Narragansetts. With the further help of Cutshamekin the Massachusetts Bay Colony coerced the Narragansetts into signing a treaty in which they agreed to break with the Pequots and join with the colony in its efforts against them.

Since one of their own had been slain (not to mention the fact the English had decimated Pequot corn fields and settlements on the Connecticut River and thus violated a treaty with the Pequot), the Pequots felt obliged to drop their policy of non-violence toward the English and they attacked Fort Saybrook in Connecticut. Soon the Puritans characterized the conflict as a battle between God and the Devil, and you know who represented whom.

The Pequots as agents of Satan had to be crushed. The focus of the English attack was their village fort, later known as Mystic, Connecticut, and the ringleaders were Captains John Underhill and John Mason, both of whom have left revealing reports of the massacre there. I have often found it noteworthy that in any war each side claims the providence of its own versions of the divine being. The Massachusetts Puritans, far from being mere examples of this practice, made it part and parcel of their entire lives, not only in war but also in all their daily activities.

Captain Underhill writes that as he and his men approached the sleeping Pequot fort they "yielded up ourselves to God and entreated his assistance in so weighty an enterprise." With him were "about three hundred" Narragansett and Mohegan Indians, all fairly reluctant, and, in any case, according to Underhill their war methods were so ineffectual "they might fight seven years and not kill seven men." Not so with the Englishmen. They were brutal almost beyond imagination. I doubt that any of the contingents now fighting for either the North or the South have been so collectively brutal to women, children, and the infirm. To attack a village by surprise and while the villagers were sleeping "bred," writes Underhill, in the Indians "such a terror that they brake forth into a most doleful cry, so as if God had not fitted the hearts of men for the service, it would have bred in them a commiseration towards them." But there was no such commiseration, for "every man being bereaved of pity fell upon the work without compassion . . . ." Underhill grants that the Pequots "behaved themselves" very "courageously," as he and Mason set the entire village afire: "Many were burnt in the fort, both men and women, and children. Others forced out, and came in troops to the Indians, twenty and thirty at a time, which our soldiers received and entertained with the point of the sword; down fell men, women, and children." Of "about four hundred souls in this fort," Underhill estimates but five escapees. Mason puts the number at "about seven."

Of the two captains, only Underhill considers the question I would expect a true Christian to consider: "Should not Christians have more mercy and compassion?" His answer to his own question? He refers the reader to "David's war" and concludes: "Sometimes the scripture declareth women and children must perish with their parents; sometime the case alters. But we will not dispute it now. We had sufficient light for the word of God for our proceedings." King David, I need not remind the reader, was *not* a Christian, and I wonder what Captain Underhill would say to some other of the Old Testament scriptures. For example, Leviticus 19: 34: "But the stranger that dwelleth with you shall be unto you as one born among you, and thou shalt love him as thyself; for ye were strangers in the land of Egypt. . . ." (I am certain Aunt Huldah is not thinking of *this* part of Leviticus when she comes to haunt me at night.) Captain Underhill would probably say that the Indians had given their "seed unto Molech." But who is the proper judge? Does not the same scripture say, "Thou shalt not kill" and "Thou shalt not bear false witness against thy neighbor" as they did in blaming the Pequots for the murders of Stone and Oldham? If they were to follow the Old Testament, would the Puritans not drain the blood of all animals before they ate them, would they not follow all the intricate laws regarding sacrifice, clothing, etc.? Did not that Puritan captive of the Indians during King Philip's War, Mistress Mary Rowlandson, eat meat with blood when she was nearly starving to death, that is, a piece of horse-liver, "not half ready"? "I was fain to take the rest," she writes in her famous memoir, "and eat it as it was with the blood about my mouth, and yet a savoury bit it was to me. . . ."

And what of the words of the New Testament, the words of Christ: "whosoever shall smite thee on thy right cheek, turn to him the other also" and "Love your enemies, bless them that curse you, do good to them that hate you, and pray for them which despitefully use you, and persecute you. . . ."? What of Christ's admonition: "all they that take the sword shall perish with the sword"? or His words on the mount: "Blessed are the meek: for they shall inherit the earth." And "Blessed are the peacemakers: for they shall be called the children of God"? Although I do not think he was a practicing Christian, I trust Mr. Hawthorne would have asked questions similar to mine. I am sure I can say the same for our great American philosopher, Henry David Thoreau.

But to the Pequot War. Even the Indian allies of the English, according to Underhill, thought their massacre too severe: "'*Mach it, mach it,*'" they said, "that is, 'It is naught, it is naught, because it is too furious and slays too many men.'" Captain Mason is, if possible, even more arrogant than is Captain Underhill. Writing of the Pequots, he says, "But God was above them, who laughed his enemies and the enemies of

135

his people to scorn, making them as a fiery oven. Thus were the stout-hearted spoiled, having slept their last sleep, and none of their men could find their hands. Thus did the Lord judge among the heathen, filling the place with dead bodies!" Instead of the four hundred slain estimated by Underhill, Mason estimates "six or seven hundred" and only two Englishmen slain, all in the space of an hour or less.

And what does the esteemed historian of Plymouth Plantation, Mr. Bradford, have to say about these matters? In his history of the plantation, he writes: "the Pequots . . . sought to make peace with the Narragansetts, and used very pernicious arguments to move them thereunto: as that the English were strangers and began to overspread their country, and would deprive them thereof in time, if they were suffered to grow and increase." If these arguments were "pernicious," they were nonetheless true, as history, alas, has demonstrated. Typically, Bradford entirely ignores the slaughter of women and children. He writes as if only Pequot warriors were at Mystic Fort (in this regard Mason and Underhill have more integrity than the renowned Plymouth historian), concluding: "the victory seemed a sweet sacrifice, and they gave the praise thereof to God, who had wrought so wonderfully for them, thus to enclose their enemies in their hands and give them so speedy a victory over so proud and insulting an enemy."

That was the end, literally, of the Pequot tribe. Those who escaped ran as far as their feet could take them. Among these were the great Pequot chief, Sassacus (a man in his seventies), who had the misfortune of trusting the Mohawks, who relieved him of his head. Others of the Pequots got away. Of those who were not so fortunate, the Puritans executed a great number of the men; the others, including women and children, were forced into slavery among the

English colonists or the Mohegans and Narragansetts, or they were sold into slavery in the West Indies. The fate of the Pequots was sealed by the Treaty of Hartford in 1638. It declared the Pequot nation defunct.

Why are the pages describing this contemptible episode in our colonial history missing from my ancestor's memoir? I hardly think it was due to any guilt on the part of Giles Hopkins or culpability on the part of his father or his brother, Caleb. True, they signed up as volunteers for the war, but they were never called, and for once Stephen Hopkins had no leadership rôle vis-à-vis the Indians, although he was one of those who was chosen to evaluate the various abilities of the volunteer soldiers. I notice in the *Plymouth Colony Records* John Cooke is on the same list of volunteers as are Giles and Caleb. In light of Giles's stated change in attitude towards John, whose brother Jacob later married Giles's sister, Damaris, I wonder whether that has anything to do with the gap in Giles's manuscript. I think not. Plymouth played no direct part in the Pequot War, unlike the war named after King Philip, which occurred long after Stephen and Caleb were dead, and Giles was too old to fight. If they felt guilty doing what would have been regarded as their civic duty, theirs was merely a crime of intent (and indeed, Caleb was only fourteen or fifteen at the time). I confess I do not know the answer to my question. Perhaps the pages in Giles's manuscript were destroyed by one of those unfortunate accidents that occasionally plague the children of Adam and Eve.

19 AUGUST 1864, EARLY PLYMOUTH ARCHITECTURE AND THE SPARROWS

SINCE MY ANCESTOR says nothing about the houses he lived in after the first years in Plymouth Plantation, perhaps I ought to tell the reader unfamiliar with our southern New England colonial houses a little about them. The house Stephen Hopkins built in Yarmouth and gave to his son Giles no longer stands, but I have been to Plymouth and, although the Hopkins house there also no longer stands, one of his epoch does: the Richard Sparrow House. Indeed, this house plays an important role in the history of my family, for the youngest sister of Giles, Elizabeth, went to live there when, after the deaths of their parents, Richard and Pandora Sparrow took her in. She was only about twelve years of age. I gather that Captain Standish, a witness to the will of Stephen Hopkins, had a hand in this adoption (or servitude?), for in 1656, after Sparrow had moved to Eastham, Standish brought an action against Sparrow for not living up to the terms "of an agreement made with the said Richard Sparrow concerning the said Elizabeth Hopkins."

By 1659 it appears Elizabeth had disappeared, having never married. Her in-laws, Andrew Ring and Jacob Cooke, and Giles, her brother, came to an "agreement" regarding her property on the 5th of October 1659 if "Elizabeth hopkins Doe Come Noe more." How cold these bare facts from the colony records are. They omit the essence, as it were: those aspects of character and emotions I should like to know. How did Giles feel about losing yet another sister, and she, the youngest, named after the eldest, whom he also lost, but with the surety of death versus the uncertainty of disappearance. Perhaps a hint of his sentiments may be suggested by the fact that he named his own youngest (and tenth) child Elizabeth. She too died before her time, only a month after her birth.

Richard and Pandora Sparrow had but one child, Jonathan, and the addition of Elizabeth Hopkins to their household, along with Mary Moorecock, who was apprenticed for nine years in 1636 to the Sparrows, provided needed workers in the family.

Again I have digressed. I was going to tell you about the Sparrow House. That it is an exact replica of the Hopkins house I doubt, for Hopkins was by 1640, the time the Sparrow House is dated, a prosperous freeman of the colony, whereas Sparrow had been in Plymouth only seven years. In 1636 he had acquired six acres of land upon which he was required to build a house in four years. I am no architect, yet I can tell you what I saw. The two-story house has but one room for each story and a lean-to, giving it another room in the back. It is what I believe is called "saltbox" construction, with clapboards for outside walls and a wood-plank roof. The windows, which are small, are glass with crisscrossed lead gridirons that somehow escaped destruction during the American Revolution, when such gridirons were dismantled so that the lead could be used for bullets. Perhaps they *were* dismantled and later restored. The floors are wooden, as are the interior walls. The ceilings have cross beams ("summer beam construction," someone said it is called). Each story has a brick fireplace, the larger being the one downstairs. Because of the size of his family, and his relative wealth, I believe Stephen Hopkins would have had a larger house, perhaps one of the kind called "hall and parlor," with a central fireplace, rooms on both sides, lofts or a second story, and a lean-to.

1607-1638, LONDON AND PLYMOUTH, INCIDENTS IN THE LIFE OF STEPHEN HOPKINS, FROM THE MEMOIR OF GILES HOPKINS

I DO NOT know whether Giles Hopkins intended to write his history in chronological order. If he had such an intention, the place where his manuscript continues after the unfortunate lacuna caused by intention or accident is rather odd. A mood to reminisce about his father, with a nod to his mother, seems to have taken hold of him. I remind my reader that my transcription endeavors not to change the words or thoughts of my ancestor, Giles, but only to render his words into modern English so far as I am capable. His hand is fairly easy to decipher. Here the manuscript begins again. Written in a different shade of ink but in the same hand just before the word "shopkeeper" are the words, "My late, lamented mother, Mary, was in England a" and then:

shopkeeper, a trade learned by her from our father to provide her a living whilst he was gone to America to seek a better situation for the family. She was a stout-hearted woman, as capable of managing a shop as any man might have been. But she died, and we children were put into the hands of Misters Lyte and Syms, the court operating under the assumption that our father had died on the high seas. These were the first of many deprivations in my life, about many of which I have already writ[ten].

The joy occasioned by my father's return from adventures, to which I have alluded, in the Bermudas and in the New World colony of Jamestown, ["Virginia" is added after this] was dampened by the loss of my sister, Elizabeth, and our removal from the Old World to the New. There, as I have revealed, my father was chosen as an ambassador, so to speak, to the Indians of the country at Patuxet, as they called it, or New Plymouth, as we English called it.

Our father's close relations to the Indians and our proximity to them in the persons of Squanto, first, and then Hobbamock and his family, second, allowed for me and later my younger brother Caleb, born in Plymouth after Squanto's passing, to become better acquainted with the savages, as our English neighbors called them. We certainly knew them better than those same neighbors. This led to both joy and sorrow, as I shall reveal at the appropriate time.

Father's familiarity with the "People of the Dawn," the Wampanoag, as they are presently known, led, I believe, to his election as assistant to the governor during the years 1633 to 1636, when he was charged with the trade in beaver skins, corn, beads, etc., with the Indians. Yet, to write with that candor which both my father and mother and the Church inculcated into me, I must say my father was at times too quick to anger, so much so that even as a governing council member he did attack and seriously hurt one John Tisdale, an ordinary yeoman, who consequently filed a complaint of battery in the court against my father, who had to pay five pounds sterling to the government for having broken the king's peace, together with forty shillings to Tisdale. The court, as I remember, added an extra censure, to the effect that he, my father, "ought after a special manner to have kept" such peace because he was himself a government official.

Since none of you, my children, save perchance my firstborn, Mary, named after my dearly departed mother, remember your grandfather, I should, methinks, add to the knowledge of him, both good and bad, I have already provided. A gentleman with, as I have revealed, a quick temper, he was also most generous, giving me, as I you know, the house he built at Yarmouth, the first house built by an Englishman there. Do you also know he did build the first wharf at Plymouth? An astute man of business, he did sell the wharf at profit for £60 in July 1637.

Yet he ever remained a "stranger," in name if not in fact, to the Separatists, who held the true and actual power in the colony, which did value him for his capabilities and experience but did not forbear to charge him with any malfeasance when he was both in and out of office. I am happy to say my father never failed in the performance of his sundry expeditions and offices, such as his assistantships to the governors and his service as a juror, yet I own he had other failings, according to colony policy and law.

I have told you of the case involving the unfortunate John Tisdale. There are other cases, perchance not as impetuous, but nevertheless revealing as to the character of your grandfather. As I have written, he was a man of business, as ye must appreciate from your comfortable upbringing. To support himself and his family, he purchased a license to sell beer and strong drink at our house. From thence resulted a number of infractions of the law. My father was charged for allowing William Reynolds to become so drunk he did vomit in a brutish manner beneath the table. For that charge Father was let off, although Mr. Reynolds was fined.

Father was not let off from numerous other charges, viz., of allowing men to drink on the Sabbath in his house whilst the meeting was yet in session, allowing other men and women to drink more than they needed for natural refreshment, for allowing servants and others to drink in his house (thus disobeying court orders to the contrary), and suffering them to play shovel board and other games. For the latter two offenses Father was fined forty shillings. A man of generous sentiments, Father saw no reason servants should not be allowed some refreshment and pleasure at games away from their masters' houses.

Yet, as I said, he was a man of business and would obtain a profit on his investment when he could. The court fined my father for selling sundry items (wine, beer, spirits, nutmegs, and a looking glass) for excessive prices, higher than those at Massachusetts Bay, and for selling the strong water after his license had expired.

Father was also involved in a more serious matter, the sorry case of Dorothy Temple, a servant of his, and her paramour, Arthur Peach, hanged for the murder of the Narragansett Indian, Penowanyanquis, on the highway at Misquamsqueece, and the theft from Penowanyanquis of three woolen coats and five fathom of wampum. Peach, who had already slain Indians in the Pequot War, had come from Virginia to Plymouth, where he induced three servants, Thomas Jackson, Richard Stinnings, and Daniel Cross, to flee from Plymouth for better prospects in the Dutch colony.

As they fled through the forest, they came upon young Penowanyanquis, whom they discovered had been trading in the Massachusetts Bay Colony and had in his possession the said stolen items. The next day, seeing the Indian again and persuading his companions to join him, Peach lured Penowanyanquis with an offer to smoke some tobacco. After they had sat down and begun to smoke, Peach waylaid Penowanyanquis by thrusting his sword twice through his body. The culprits, thinking their victim dead, stole off.

The victim, however, was not yet dead and was found by another Indian and taken to Roger Williams, who soon was faced with angry Narragansetts declaring what the Pequots had said was true, viz., that the English would hunt them down piecemeal and kill them. Doctors were brought in to attend Penowanyanquis, but they found his wounds mortal. Before he died, the young Narragansett told Williams and the others what had happened and identified the men. While this was happening, the Indians had caught the men, all but Daniel Cross, who had escaped.

The authorities in Plymouth tried to have the charges against the three brought against them in Boston, but the Massachusetts Bay officials said the jurisdiction belonged to Plymouth, where the assassins had last resided. Thomas Prence, then governor, and his council knew, despite arguments to the contrary to the effect that no white man should die for killing an Indian, that any show of partiality towards these three white men would arouse serious trouble from the Indians so soon after the Pequot affair. A jury was selected, and the men were tried and hanged directly in the presence of the village and a few of the Narragansetts, who were satisfied justice had been done.

But the story does not end there. Not long after the hangings, it became apparent that my father's maid servant, Dorothy Temple, was with child. When questioned, she identified the father as none other than the lately executed Arthur Peach. Mother declared she was not surprised, for Peach had called on Dorothy numerous times. My father was not, as you should know by now, a man who kept scrupulously to the law. He might have forgiven his servant her transgression had her paramour been any other than Arthur Peach, a vile thief and Indian killer, who, furthermore, was not liked by Mother. (And, I think, he did not want the additional burden of a child in the house.) Father attempted to free himself from his contract with Dorothy Temple, for which the court imprisoned him in his own house till he changed his mind. John Holmes, the court messenger, agreed to accept Dorothy and her baby until the term of her indenture was finished. Father agreed to pay £3 for her expenses. When Dorothy's child, a "male bastard," in the phrase of the court, was born, she was whipt, according to the sentence of the court. The sentence was that she be whipt twice, but having fainted during the first whipping, she was spared a second.

1642-44, Stephen Hopkins and Jonathan Hatch, etc., from the Memoir of Giles Hopkins

NOW, MY CHILDREN, since I have endeavored to tell the truth in these memoirs, I must tell ye of a most unsavory entanglement in which your grandfather was involved, albeit only in a beneficial rôle. Be patient, and tolerant, as I try to recall and untangle this inordinately bizarre and sickening case. I was living in Yarmouth with your mother at the time of these events, yet they were so noised about nobody in the colony could have been ignorant of them, and indeed, there was such a gathering at and in the court when the charges were brought against the parties it seemed like a holiday I was told; the same can be said as you shall see, I am sorry to say, for the times the sentences against the various persons were carried out. The humiliation these criminals received, I suppose, was intended by the government when it passed the laws and by the court when it ordered the punishments to be carried out in public. They were meant to be exemplary.

145

The persons involved were the following: Lydia Hatch, her brother, Jonathan Hatch, Edward Mitchell, Edward Preston, and John Keene. Lydia Hatch was charged with fornication because she did allow Edward Mitchell to know her (to use the Biblical word) in an unclean manner. She was also charged for lying in bed with her brother, Jonathan. For these offenses she was whipt in public.

Edward Mitchell was charged not only for his "lude carriages with Lydia," as the court would phrase it, but also for his lewd practices which tended toward sodomy with Edward Preston. For these charges Mitchell was convicted and sentenced to be whipt in public at Plymouth and at Barnstable in the presence of the governing committees of that town. I admit, my children, I was present to witness the humiliation and suffering of Mitchell and Preston at Plymouth. It was a vexing spectacle to see the people of Plymouth so vicious. The people, some of them drink drunk, yelled epithets at the criminals (for Preston was whipt at the same time as was Mitchell). "Filthy swine," "Unnatural villains," "vile sodomites," were such phrases as the crowd flung at these two, yet I reckon their crimes merited the punishment.

Edward Preston, for his compliance with Mitchell together with his attempt to entice John Keene to do the same (though he was found not to have given in to the temptation) was whipt also at Plymouth, as I have said, and at Barnstable at the same time Edward Mitchell was whipt. Keene, for not having yielded to the temptation and for reporting it to the authorities, was ordered to watch whilst Preston and Mitchell were both whipt, this because, I suspect, the court thought him as guilty as the other parties but no proof was provided of such suspicion.

You may wonder what part does my father, Stephen Hopkins, play in this case. Be patient, my children. I am going to tell you now. He it was who agreed by the court's consent to take in Jonathan Hatch after his, Hatch's, having been whipt for vagrancy and other misdemeanors, but strangely not, I should tell ye, for incest. I have wondered, as perchance ye are now wondering, why Father in the last two or three years of his life would agree to take into his care such an unsavory character as this Jonathan Hatch. Perhaps Father was lonely, for his beloved wife Elizabeth had died and he had only Caleb and his unmarried daughters to comfort him. Yet I wonder whether because of Jonathan's character Father came to regret having Jonathan in the house.

Yes, I knew him, and his charming personality was matched only by his well-favored good looks. But these are no reasons to take a criminal into your home. A year or so before his conviction in the case I have described, Jonathan was punished by the court for slandering a Mr. Nicholas Sympkins, saying falsely he had tried to lie with his Indian maid servant. I wonder whether Jonathan himself had lain with the woman. Perhaps the court suspected the same. He was one of those in whom the natural (and I believe the unnatural) urges were stronger than they are in the general run of men. He had a sort of appeal that, dare I say it, attracted those around him. My brother Caleb felt it I am sure; perchance my sisters felt it. Even I was not exempt from his charms. Had I known his past and future history I might not have found him so beguiling.

1644-1676, JONATHAN HATCH AND OTHERS, FROM THE MEMOIR OF GILES HOPKINS

AFTER FATHER DIED in 1644, I kept an eye on Jonathan. This was not difficult, for I have had acquaintance of numerous members of the grand juries of Plymouth throughout the years. As you know, their duty was to scrutinize the activities of their neighbors. That is why I know he joined the soldiers from Barnstable in 1645, recruited for a possible skirmish with the Narragansetts over the murder of their sachem, Miantonomo, in a conspiracy with the Mohegans, under their sachem, Uncas, and the United Colonies (Massachusetts Bay, Connecticut, New Haven, and Plymouth). Fortunately, that dispute was settled without violence. In 1651 Jonathan was acquitted of having hired Indian land, but some fourteen or fifteen years later he was convicted of unnecessarily frequenting the house of Thomas Crippin. The court suspected him of tempting Frances Crippin, wife of Thomas, to commit lewd acts. It did forbid him to arouse such suspicion at that house or to be seen in the company of Frances.

His infractions, so far as I know of them, do not end there. In 1670 he was fined by the court for selling strong drink to the Indians. Finally, I know that after King Philip's War Jonathan Hatch did purchase two Indians, a man and wife, and a young Indian man. He has told me he intends to sell them back to the Indians in a short time, apart from the young man, whom he will keep for a few years until he reaches the age of twenty-four. He has also told me of his ambition to open an ordinary so that he may sell beer and strong drink for the refreshment of those who would stop at his establishment.

Knowing my father, I believe Jonathan convinced him of his intentions to do better for the future and of his love and concern for the Indians. Also, as I have said, Father would have welcomed a new person into the house after the death of his wife, and Jonathan would have been an extra worker in his fields.

I must tell ye also that the punishments meted out to the sodomites Mitchell and Preston were light compared to what they could have by law received. The law provided for the hanging of anyone convicted of sodomy, and I think the only reason that punishment was not enforced was that the colony did not have a royal patent. Therefore, wicked men such as John Alexander and Thomas Roberts, whose lascivious and unclean behavior toward each other and their frequent wasting of their seed on one another resulted in their convictions for sodomy, were spared the ultimate penalty and instead, in the case of Alexander, a notorious sodomite and seducer of others to his evil ways, was merely whipt severely, branded with a hot iron in his shoulder, and banished forever from the colony under penalty of whipping if ever he be found there again. Roberts, an indentured servant to a Mr. Atwood, was only whipt severely and returned to his master to serve out his term but without promise of land at the end of that term, unless he reformed his ways. Had either of these perverted brutes lived in the Massachusetts Bay Colony, they surely would have been hanged, as I know such happened to another young servant of perhaps eighteen to twenty years of age.

1642, THOMAS GRANGER HANGED FOR BUGGERY IN PLYMOUTH, FROM THE MEMOIR OF GILES HOPKINS

NOW, CHILDREN, I trust when ye read this you will all be of sufficient age and maturity (for the two are not identical, as I have endeavored to teach you) to remain untainted by what I have now to write. Plymouth Colony, while lenient to sodomites, was not as lenient toward buggery, at least concerning its first known appearance in the colony. Thus the lamentable case of one Thomas Granger, a servant to Love Brewster in Duxbury of about age sixteen or seventeen years. Granger had been put out by his parents, who lived in Scituate, at an early age. He was convicted of buggery with a number of beasts, among them a mare (with which his lewd business was the first witnessed by another), a cow, goats, sheep, calves, and a turkey.

Upon first being accused of his actions, the somewhat dim-witted boy denied them. When presented with witnesses to his unspeakable crimes, he recanted and confessed to the point of identifying which animals he did commit his unclean acts with. They paraded the animals before him and he had said, "No, no, never with her." "Aye, yes there's the one; we were ever so tight." You could hear a loud gasp when he said that. I was there, as were my father and my brother, Caleb.

Governor Bradford said it was a sad yet foul case, but there was nothing he and the court could do but condemn the boy as the law prescribed in Leviticus 20: 15: "And if a man lie with a beast, he shall surely be put to death: and ye shall slay the beast." So each of the eight guilty animals was butchered as young Thomas Granger watched, later to be buried without any use made of them in a large pit, and then Granger himself was hanged.

Father, for one, was deeply angered. For one, he said, Granger was only a boy and not a very shrewd boy at that. For another, if they were going to base their laws on Moses, as they claimed to be doing, he wanted to know "why they are not sacrificing bulls on the altar, why they do not execute those that work on the Sabbath (he himself might have been one of these), why they eat shell fish, even eagles we ate when we first settled here,--all forbidden by the law of Moses, never mind rabbits and swine. Why indeed do they not murder those who blasphemy as the Scriptures enjoin? Or plant their fields with a single seed and never mingle a garment with linen and wool?" Father was so angry that day Caleb and I were too fearful to question him. We remained silent as he spoke to his friend, the governor, about his objections.

"My dear Hopkins," said Bradford. "We have not proceeded lightly nor without great deliberation and counsel from our ministers."

"But the poor boy was daft. Anybody could see that."

"I doubt not it was an awful ordeal for all of us. Let us take care that our servants be instructed in holiness and keep the Sabbath regularly."

Father's face had turned that color of red which foretold an altercation that could do nothing but get him into trouble. With all the tact I could muster, I called him away from the governor, his longtime friend and spiritual antagonist.

22 OCTOBER 1864, EASTHAM, CAPE COD (SEXUAL CRIMES IN EARLY PLYMOUTH; THE PUNISHMENTS FOR SUCH CRIMES; THE USE OF TORTURE, ETC.)

HERE I MIGHT interrupt Giles again to offer the fruit of some of my own research on the subjects he mentions. My ancestor, though he knew him in the flesh, had not the advantage of a copy of Governor Bradford's history of Plymouth Plantation, as he styled it. That appeared in print only some eight years ago, in, that is, 1856. Giles would have known about the first case of adultery to have presented itself to the Plymouth court, that in which Mary, wife of Robert Mendame from Duxbury, was charged with having committed adultery with an Indian called Tinsin. Now in the Old Testament adultery was a capital crime, as the harshest of the three ministers Bradford refers to, Mr. Charles Chauncy, points out, yet in Plymouth, unlike the Massachusetts Bay Colony, no one was ever put to death for the crime of adultery. Instead, Mrs. Mendame was sentenced, and I quote from the *Plymouth Colony Records*, "to be whipt at a carts tayle through the townes streets, and to weare a badge [with the letters "AD" for adultery] upon her left sleeve during her aboad within this goverment; and if shee shalbe found without it abroad, then to be burned in the face with a hott iron." (As the reader can plainly see, I have not corrected the spelling and punctuation as I have in Giles's manuscript. I thought it best to preserve the spirit of the court's judgement, so unlike our enlightened judiciary of today.) Because he was deemed to have been the victim of "allurement" and "inticement," Tinsin's sentence was slightly less severe: "to be well whipt with a halter about his neck at the post." Also, because he was an Indian, Tinsin was deemed to have an inferior understanding of God's moral law. I believe the late, lamented Mr. Hawthorne must have got some of the inspiration for his great work, *The Scarlet Letter*, from this sentence and others like it.

While surely familiar with this and the many other instances of sexual crimes in Plymouth Colony, if not in Massachusetts Bay Colony, if I am not mistaken, Giles Hopkins could not have been privy to the thoughts of the conscientious governor as he wrote them in his history. All of the ministers whose counsel he sought and whose letters he inserts, all of them, the Revs. John Rayner, Ralph Partridge, and Charles Chauncy, considered sodomy a capital offense, even if, despite Bradford's opinion to the contrary, there was no penetration ("*cum penetratione corporis,*" to quote the learned Rev. Rayner). Only Rev. Partridge has doubts on this score. As I have pointed out, the most Rev. Chauncy is the harshest (and, I might add, the most loquacious) on this and many other "unnatural vices,": "rape, incest, bestiality, unnatural sins, presumptuous sins," among which he includes "destroying conception in the womb by potions," though he admits there is no scripture proscribing such. As for "Onan's sin," or "*an contactus et fricatio,*" he theorizes that, like the latter, we may by analogy detect it as indeed a sin. He then quotes a lengthy passage in Latin from Pareus, which I shall spare the reader because it does not pertain directly to my story, based on the papers I have found in the attic of my aunt. If you wish to read it, I recommend your finding a copy of Gov. Bradford's history. Boston would be a fine place to start your search.

However, I can not help but find it pertinent that all three of these Puritan divines opposed torture as a means of gaining confession for unnatural sins. Again, Chauncy somewhat differs from the other two ministers of the Gospel, for he writes:

> But now, if the question be meant of inflicting
> bodily torments to extract a confession from a
> malefactor, I conceive that in matters of highest
> consequence, such as do concern the safety or
> ruin of states or countries, magistrates may
> proceed so far to bodily torments, as racks, hot
> irons, etc. to extract a confession, especially
> where presumptions are strong; but otherwise
> by no means. God sometimes hides a sinner till
> his wickedness is filled up.

I presume the good reverend, if he were as logical as he purports to be, would not have condemned the use of torture by the Indians on their prisoners of war (except that they, the Indians, by virtue of their not being Christians, may fall outside the purview of the reverend's logic).

Pardon me, dear reader, I am, I fear, guilty again of my besetting literary sin: digression. Like you (and again I presume; forgive me), I am horrified at the sexual crimes or sins our forefathers worried so much about. (And I feel certain none of my ancestors were truly guilty of similar crimes, despite certain equivocal statements by Giles Hopkins I have transcribed.) On the other hand, compared to the great civil war now going on, and all the consequent carnage both sides have endured and doubtless will endure, such crimes seem, if not trivial, certainly not urgent in their gravity. I am sure our great authors, particularly Walt Whitman, would agree with me.

My brother, James, and my sister, Sarah, whose advice I have sometimes sought regarding these papers, have questioned whether I ought to have written about the sexual crimes of Plymouth. Of course, I have not consulted my nephews Paul and Silas on these matters. In the interests of truth, I told James and Sarah, I must discuss the opinions and actions of our Plymouth forefathers, whether direct ancestors or not.

Now, to prevent further digression on my part, I return to the narrative of Giles Hopkins:

1639, THE CIVIL MARRIAGE OF GILES HOPKINS AND CATHERINE WHELDEN, FROM THE MEMOIR OF GILES HOPKINS

I HAVE NEGLECTED to iterate the story of my marriage to your beloved mother, Catherine, because I think ye are familiar with it already, our anniversary, 9th October 1639, being a cause for remembrance annually. Ye know enough about my attitudes, instilled through long experience and the example of my father, to know why I could break custom (if not the law, for no law forbids marriage with the Indians) and marry a woman whose mother was not only an Indian of the Wampanoag tribe but indeed the daughter of one whose place in its history is one of prominence and honor. I mean, of course, the great sachem, Quadequina, brother of Massasoit.

Because of the severe strictures of the Separatists, who believe marriage is no sacrament (they allow only two: baptism and the Lord's Supper), we had no church wedding but a mere civil ceremony, performed by the magistrate at Plymouth, for in 1639 we had none at Yarmouth. Father and Mother, she being of course my stepmother, did not hesitate to bless our union (and I, being well over thirty years of age, asked for their permission merely out of respect for the

155

scriptural command to honour thy father and mother). Your mother, however, was not of age, being sixteen at the time, yet anyone could see we loved each other, and her father, happy to make an alliance with our family, readily agreed to our marriage. For what our neighbors thought I cared little, having lived for years in Plymouth with the smirks and the overheard innuendoes whispered about regarding my family's close relationships with the family of Hobbamock, and especially, for me, with Netop. In a word, I did not care for the approval of my neighbors yet, I believe, they did come to fully accept my marriage with your mother for, as ye know, she has that feminine knack to make strangers and neighbors feel welcome and comfortable in her presence.

Her late father, as ye are well aware, eventually sold the property in Nottinghamshire, Old England, which he owned with his brother Ralph. After that, Gabriel, ever a restless spirit, took himself and his wife, Margaret, to Malden, where they both did die. Father provided for Catherine and me the house he built in Yarmouth and the land surrounding it. But of recent family history ye have no especial need to hear. Ye know it already.

CHAPTER SIX
A BRIEF HISTORY OF JOHN COOKE
& HIS ANABAPTIST HERESY,
OTHER RELIGIOUS DISPUTES AT PLYMOUTH,
A CONFESSION BY GILES HOPKINS,
THE DEATH OF STEPHEN HOPKINS,
AND
THE HISTORY OF HIS DAUGHTER, RUTH

3 JANUARY 1865, EASTHAM, CAPE COD

I CONFESS I set aside my labor of love transcribing the Plymouth Papers, as I like to call them, to celebrate the Christmas and New Year holidays with the family of my brother and sister-in-law. This time my sister and her family were also able to join us here in Eastham, probably for the last time, although now my brother and sister are suggesting I keep the house and rent it, dividing the rents into three equal portions. I shall see.

Sarah has two fine young daughters, Emily and Charlotte, aged nine and seven. They are always welcome at my gatherings, though I confess I get a little nervous when they play their girlish games and otherwise titter about the house. They have a long way to go before they reach the maturity of my nephew, Paul. Silas, on the other hand, still has some growing to do. I try to act the good uncle to each of them, not always successfully, I fear.

Nevertheless, the holidays went splendidly. Sarah helped prepare the Christmas supper. We had turkey, dressing, potatoes, baked clams, biscuits, chowder, of course, cranberries from Plymouth, and pumpkin pie, which Sarah's girls made themselves, proving they are good for something, after all. Although I made the hot cider, we also had mulled wine, praying the forgiveness of the late proprietress of the house, whose ghostly visitations have all but ceased, I might add, to my great relief.

I should tell you that I celebrate Christmas not for any particular religious reasons. As you know, I am a rationalist who, while believing in the moral principles of Christ, relies on modern science for my guide to knowledge. I am of the church of Emerson and Thoreau, an American individualist. I do not believe the God of Nature or Providence, if you please, will think less of me for that. A bachelor, I was 47 when the present civil war commenced and therefore too old for duty, I am pleased to report. (I might add that I am particularly grateful my nephews are too young to fight in the war.)

My dear aunt passed on, and I, being executor of her will, discovered these papers, which have consumed too much time away from my business as a publisher. My present intention is to publish these papers with a larger firm when an appropriate period of time has passed after the end of the war, which, I need not add, I sincerely hope will be soon. If I can't find a larger firm to publish my book, I will publish it myself.

The memoirs of Giles Hopkins confirm what I already knew, that the "Pilgrims" were a mean, stubborn, and intolerant lot. But let the words of Giles speak for themselves:

1603-1670, JOHN COOKE, HIS ANABAPTISM, AND A BRIEF HISTORY OF THE SEPARATISTS, FROM THE MEMOIR OF GILES HOPKINS

THE NAME OF my erstwhile friend, John Cooke, has appeared often enough in this history that I think ye may wish to know what has become of him. Since his history reveals much about the history of Plymouth Colony, I think a slight summary of John's personal history would not be inappropriate.

Thus far ye have seen how the opinions of your grandfather and mine own have strayed from those of the Separatist leaders of our colony. In some ways, we were on more congenial terms with the Indians, not condemning, for the most part, what Gov. Bradford, Ed[ward] Winslow, and others called their heathenism. I think Father was more inclined than I to accept the opinions of these Separatists. Be that as it may, John Cooke, as I have told you, was inclined toward the Separatists' views. He was one of them, baptized in Leyden, Holland, where they had taken refuge from English persecution. So dedicated was he to the church of these Separatist Puritans, he became a deacon in the congregation in our Plymouth church. Neither Father nor Mother nor I ever became a member of that church. We were always of the Church of England, but conformed so far as conscience would allow to the strictures of the Separatists.

Perhaps I should reprise briefly the ecclesiastical history of Old and New England (or that part of New England in which ye have been born and reared). You know that in the sixteenth century King Henry VIII broke away from the Roman church and founded the Church of England, of which since then the reigning monarch has been the head. In Europe, too, Martin Luther and John Calvin were leading the Reformation away from the hideous errors of popery. In southern and western Germany, Switzerland, Holland, Moravia, and Austria men such as Obbe Philips, Menno Simons, and Conrad Grebel led Protestant Christians into what both the Catholics and the other Protestants considered the heresy of Anabaptism (also called, under Grebel and others, the "Brethren"), meaning the belief that those who had been baptized as infants needed to be baptized again as adults after a confession of personal faith in our Lord, Jesus Christ. To them, infant baptism signified nothing.

In England, the people we know as Puritans believed the Church of England might as well have been Catholic but for the lack of a pope. They wished to "purify" the church from ecclesiastical courts, priestly vestments, altars, and kneeling during the mass. They believed reform could be accomplished within the church itself whilst the Separatists believed not; they, instead, wished to separate entirely from the church. They felt the church was too lax in enforcing the canons of holy scripture, such as avoiding drunkenness and keeping the Sabbath. In the mean while, when Catholic Queen Mary (viz., "Bloody Mary") took the throne, she burnt hundreds of true believers because they refused allegiance to Rome. Her half-sister, Queen Elizabeth, a Protestant, was more tolerant of dissenters, but when King James succeeded her, his persecution was such that the Separatists, to escape being burnt themselves at the stake, fled the country for Holland.

John Cooke, with whom I was friends from the time of our voyage on the *Mayflower,* came from the Separatists, his father being Francis Cooke and his mother, Hester, being the daughter of French-speaking Walloons, i.e., French Protestants. They had removed from England to Leyden,

Holland, and married there in 1603, before the main body of Separatists arrived five years thence. I believe John's close childhood proximity to the Dutch Anabaptists surely influenced his views as he grew older in Plymouth.

Jacob, John's brother and the late husband of my sister, Damaris, was born also in Leyden, but just two years before we sailed on the *Mayflower*. Jacob never converted to Anabaptism. Because of this relationship to my family, John and I have seen each other from time to time over the years, though we live in domiciles separated by many miles of forest, meadows, and water.

John had always been an earnest young man, so conscientious, as I have said, he was appointed deacon in the church. He was also an active member of the community at Dartmouth, serving as deputy and magistrate for many years. What caused him to question certain of the practices of the government and church I can not say, apart from the childhood I have noted. In addition to the belief that only confessing or believing adults should be baptized (or baptized again if they had been baptized as babies), he began to believe that the government should not be ruled by Mosaic law, that the New Testament should be the authority for all doctrine, and that indeed the government and the church ought to be separate. He cited the words of Jesus to Pilate in the scripture, John 18: 36: "My kingdom is not of this world: if my kingdom were of this world, then would my servants fight, that I should not be delivered to the Jews; but now is my kingdom not from hence." And, although he also used 2 Corinthians 5: 20 ("Now then we are ambassadors for Christ. . . .") as a basis for his belief, he served with Nathaniel Warren as an emissary to Metacom (called King Philip) in 1665 to negotiate the purchase of some land for Plymouth.

And this was after he was expelled from the church for what was called his "error" of Anabaptism in about 1658.

Certainly, he believed the Anabaptist tenet of nonresistance, meaning he would never take up arms to defend the colony (although, like his brother, Jacob, my father, Caleb, and me, he volunteered to fight the Pequots in 1637) and that executing anyone for any reason was contrary to the teachings of the New Testament. The same was true for the pernicious evil of enslavement, practiced in New England even before we came on the *Mayflower* when Englishmen like Thomas Hunt captured and sold Indians into slavery. Until the war with Metacom, very few Indians were slaves. Some few were indentured servants, as were some very few Africans. After the Pequot War, the colony sold Indians as slaves, as I have said, and the Massachusetts Bay Colony traded Pequots for African slaves. In Plymouth, besides the Indian slaves, a few colonists had black slaves as well. All of this was condemned as against the Gospel by the Anabaptists, as well as by the Quakers.

Yet even as obnoxious as such opinions were to the Separatist government, after his excommunication from the church, John was spared the sufferings meted out to others of his opinions. (Although, like the Quakers, Anabaptists refused to take Oaths of Fidelity to the colony, John was not punished as were the Quakers, who were whipt and exiled from the colony many times. In Massachusetts Bay Colony, some of them had their ears cropped or were hanged.) Indeed, not only was he a negotiator for the colony with Metacom, but also he was successful in a land dispute with Dartmouth. That my old friend was treated fairly by the court is proved by this example and the fact he was fined in 1670 for traveling on the Sabbath, so I was told. I suppose he was going to preach at a Baptist church, for he did become a preacher.

1658, THE PERSECUTION OF THE QUAKERS IN PLYMOUTH, FROM THE MEMOIR OF GILES HOPKINS

THE SEPARATISTS WERE glad to have dissenters among them as long as they attended *their* meetings on the Sabbath. They had come to the New World to find liberty to practice their own variety of the Christian religion. Yet when Anabaptists and Quakers came into their midst, they did everything they could, short of hanging them, to harass and otherwise persecute them. In addition to requiring freemen to take Oaths of Fidelity, a thing abhorrent to the Quakers, the government ordered that no resident of the colony should be hospitable to a Quaker, if he knew the person to be one. Then they took away the right of any Quaker to be a freeman, to wit: "noe Quaker Rantor or any such corrupt person shalbee admited to bee a freeman of this Corporation."

Not all the Quakers were meek when charged with being in Biblical error. Brought before Gov. Thomas Prence and the court in 1658 for having entered Plymouth when the law forbad it, Humphrey Norton and John Rouse resisted the accusations made against them. "Thow lyest," said Norton. "Thomas, thow art a mallicious man." Norton was brought to the court again and presented with a document drawn up by Christopher Winter detailing his errors. Given an opportunity to read the document, and finding it fairly inaccurate, Norton continued what in the view of the court was his insolence: "Thy clamorouse toungue I regard noe more then the dust under my feet; and thou art like a scoulding woman; and thow pratest and deridest mee."

Because both Norton and Rouse declared themselves English subjects, they were told to take the Oath of Fidelity, which of course they refused to do. Their penalty was to be whipt, yet they refused to pay the required fees for their whipping after it was done unto them. This resulted in their being returned to prison until they would pay the fees. After a few days, Norton and Rouse relented and agreed to pay the fees. They were let go.

Whether they were bold like Norton and Rouse or meek, Quakers were fined, jailed, whipt, and expelled from the colony. Yet by the early years of this decade of the 1670s, they had become ensconced in Sandwich and Dartmouth, the haven of John Cooke. Perhaps because he was a first comer he was spared the ignominy the others had suffered.

In the early years of the colony, the Separatists themselves were upbraided by the Adventurers for various shortcomings. One of them was the failure to adhere to their sacraments of infant baptism and the Lord's Supper. Gov. Bradford's reply to this was that they had no pastor to administer the sacraments. Another serious accusation, my father laughingly told me, was that children were not being catechized and taught to read. You yourselves know the falseness of that particular charge. That, I think, is sufficient on religion for the nonce.

25 JANUARY 1865, EASTHAM, CAPE COD (1624-36, THE SEARCH FOR A PASTOR IN PLYMOUTH)

HOLD ON, MY dear ancestor! Now you've piqued *my* interest in the religious leadership of Plymouth. Dear reader, you know by now what I do when my interest is aroused: I go to the library or I poke around book stores and antiquarian shops. Sometimes I find the topics I find in the books on the shelves so interesting I forget the original purpose of my journey to the library or book store. Boston is filled with such places of interest to a lover of books, and Boston itself, as you no doubt know, is the home of the Mother Church of the Christian Scientists, followers of Mary Baker Eddy. In addition to this new sect, America has spawned many new Christian religions (the Church of Jesus Christ of Latter-day Saints and the Seventh-day Adventists are but two other examples), all of which would have been anathema to the so-called "Pilgrims." Indeed, my late aunt's conversion in a camp meeting from the very church the religion of the "Pilgrims" evolved into, the Congregational Church, would have shocked them. Thousands of people attended those camp meetings, set up in enormous tents. Many ministers would preach, but usually they were led by one charismatic gentleman, such as Father Taylor (no relation to me), who preached at the services Aunt Huldah attended. Hundreds joined her in becoming believers in this more vigorous variety of Christianity, which was sneered at by the Massachusetts newspapers and magazines. How the prevailing winds of belief change! Dear reader, if you find this subject bores you, please, by all means skip ahead to the resumption of Giles's narrative.

For those of you who might like to know, here is what I learned about what I now like to call "the pastor problem at Plymouth." I shall try to be brief. I did not have to search far for what I wanted to find, since Gov. Bradford was good enough to record it for me. In 1624 a minister named John Lyford arrived from England, along with a John Oldham. At first everything seemed hunky-dory, so to speak. As is his practice, Bradford writes in the third person in his history. He declares the leaders of the colony "gave him

[Lyford] the best entertainment they could, in all simplicity, and a larger allowance of food out of the store than any other had." The gracious governor extended him counseling privileges with the likes of "their Elder, Mr. Brewster, together with his Assistants." Then followed church membership, not an easy thing to come by amongst the Separatists.

During this cozy reception, Bradford maintains, the Reverend Lyford was acting two-faced. He (the governor) quotes appropriate scripture for comparison, which I omit for the sake of brevity. He soon informs his reader that Lyford and Oldham had been plotting by means of letters to England to, in "a spirit of great malignancy," bring "as many into faction as they could," the result of which was the gathering of almost everyone into a "fool's paradise." Among the letters Bradford found were copies made by Lyford of a purloined letter written to Elder Brewster "by a gentleman in England" and one written by Edward Winslow to the Separatist pastor, John Robinson, in Holland. Lyford had put in the margins of these letters "many scurrilous and flouting annotations."

How did the astute governor know about these letters and what did he do? He and his close associates took a shallop out to the ship on which the subversive letters were to be carried to Old England and, since Bradford and the ship's master, William Peirce, were good friends, Peirce allowed Bradford to himself purloin the letters, which he promptly copied and brought back to Plymouth as evidence.

What, specifically, was the "sin" of the Misters Lyford and Oldham? They "intended a reformation in church and commonwealth, and as soon as the ship was gone, they intended to join together and have the sacraments, etc."

What horror such a spectacle must have caused our dedicated "forefathers." John Lyford may have been a reverend, but he was not a Separatist reverend. He was of the Church of England and he did indeed set up a rival church. This, it need not be said, was intolerable to Bradford and his pious cohorts, so they tried Lyford and Oldham and expelled them from the colony. The entire episode was far more complicated than I have reported it, but I promised to be brief.

You may ask, Why didn't the Rev. John Robinson come over from Holland and pastor his flock? The answer to that question is simple: he died before he could (if indeed he really wanted to). Next Isaac Allerton, one of the more troublesome of the first comers, brought back from a trip to England a young Rev. Mr. Rogers (no Christian name is given). He too was unsuitable because, as Bradford puts it, he was "crazed in his brain." He got sent back quicker than did Lyford and Oldham.

In 1629 the Rev. Ralph Smith arrived from Salem in the Bay Colony. He too proved unsuitable, albeit he stayed on till 1636, when "he laid down his place of ministry, partly by his own willingness as thinking it too heavy a burthen, and partly at the desire and by the persuasion of others." In other words, he did not make the strict Separatist grade.

I have heard it said the third time is a charm, but for these people it was the fourth. Or, strictly speaking, the sixth, for, trying to replace Rev. Smith, Edward Winslow found, in England, a Rev. Glover, but he got the fever and died before he could get on the boat. The fifth candidate for a suitable pastor was the Rev. John Norton, who came over, again at the invitation of Mr. Winslow, on a provisional basis. The Plymouth people liked him well enough, but after about a year he thought preferable the "many rich and able men and sundry of his acquaintance" at Ipswich, and there he went.

Only on their sixth attempt in 1636 to acquire an ordained minister they found acceptable were the Plymouth Puritans successful, at least for nearly twenty years (but that *is* another story). This time the minister was none other than the Rev. Mr. John Rayner, he whose views on sodomy and its just punishment you have already been made acquainted with. Of him Bradford writes: "it pleased the Lord to send them an able and a godly man . . . of a meek and humble spirit, sound in the truth and every way unreprovable in his life and conversation." Even *he* had to pass "some time of trial" before he was fully accepted by these persnickety people (forgive me another colloquialism, this one from the Scots I do believe). I gather from my research there were a number of unbaptized babies who passed on to the other side while these particular Puritans deliberated on an acceptable pastor.

Forgive yet another digression, dear reader. Here is Giles again:

1642, GILES HOPKINS FILES CHARGES AGAINST WILLIAM CARSLEY, FROM THE MEMOIR OF GILES HOPKINS

OH MY CHILDREN, I am well past the number of years my father had when he yielded to the "frail estate of all men," to use his own words. Confession, I have heard, is good for the soul, but whatever I may confess here, please to God it should not be read until I myself have yielded to the frail estate of all men. Thus I may be honest and beg God's forgiveness for all my shortcomings and sins.

I write all this by way of introduction to the sorry case of William Carsley, formerly the constable at Barnstable, a freeman, a church member in good standing, and my friend. Whether I myself was at fault in the case I can not judge these thirty-five or more years hence. I have prayed that I be forgiven for any such fault that lies at my door.

I attribute part of this, and other similar problems I shall confess in good time, to what I see as the curse of my family: our good looks. Do not smile, my children, and do not smirk. I say this not out of false pride but as a frank and godly assessment of the facts of the case, or may I say, the cases, to which I refer.

I fear I am in danger of becoming prolix in order to avoid saying what I feel I must confess. Yet it is nothing in comparison to the confession I must make before I finish this history. The full particulars of the incidents concerning the case I used my influence, such as it is, and that of my father, to expunge from the records of the colony, yet the consequences, or some of the consequences, to William are there, unexpunged, for all to see. I did keep my name out of the records, but not the general charge I brought against him, that of "unclean carriages towards men that he had lyen withall." I regretted having to bring such charges against William because he was my friend. I regretted them afterwards because of Caleb and Ruth, but more on that later.

William was not what ye would call a handsome man. He was plain, with a scraggly mouse-colored beard, unlike Father's dark and neatly trimmed beard and my moustache. William and I met at his church at Barnstable. Now I must tell ye that sexual infractions in Plymouth were not uncommon. About the time of my experiences with William, John Caseley and his wife, Alice, were charged and convicted of fornication before they had wed. He was whipt and she was put in the stocks. The same happened to many couples, and especially those whose first child came within less than the natural nine months, thus proving their guilt.

William's crime was not of that nature. He would come to me when I was in the field or persuade me to take some tobacco and a beer in the meadow for a rest and then he would stare into mine eyes as does a courting man at his woman. Thinking, I suppose, I did like such attentions because I said nothing, he proceeded to put his hand upon my leg and to kiss me on mine lips.

"Will," I said, pushing him away, "what is the meaning of this?"

His visage became red. "It was a kiss of Christian appreciation for all your kindnesses to me," was his answer.

We continued as before, talking of the weather and the growth of the corn, my new heifer and the like. I thought nothing of it.

Yet when next we met, he did the same, only this time he showed me by his bodily position that the sexual (I can not say procreational) urge in him was strong. He rubbed and pressed himself and said, "You see, I am cocked . . . cocked and ready."

This time there was no kiss, and as I got up and pretended I had to return to my work, he got himself up and departed.

After that I did not see William for some time, perhaps three or four months. I was working on the road on a hot summer day, repairing the fence, when he happened to come by on his horse. Again he suggested a period of rest in the cool of the nearby woods. He had some beer and tobacco, and I thought it no harm to join him.

Again he gave me that look, which I endeavored to ignore. I really had no reason to dislike him. He had been friendly since the time we had met. And after all he was the constable. I put his past behavior down to youthful spirits. We drank two bottles of beer and smoked a pipe of tobacco. It was beginning to make me dizzy. I said that was more than sufficient for refreshment. He smiled at me in a most peculiar way and before I knew what had happened, he was on me, his mouth at my mouth, his tongue inserted, and his hand on my private parts. He had, whilst I was not looking (I know not how) loosened his trousers, revealing the fullness of his unnatural desires.

I confess the suddenness of his action stirred in me a little of the excitement he displayed, and he must have felt that, but I was angered he should think I encouraged him in any way. With great difficulty I pushed him away and reproached him. "William!" I said. "This time ye have gone too far!"

"No," he said in a sad and muffled way.

"Yea. I shall have to report ye to the authorities and bring charges."

"Oh, no. Please, please Giles," he said. "I love thee! Yet I will not approach ye again if thou wishes it."

"Indeed, ye will not. But I have my honor to uphold. Ye have now equaled Peter's record of betrayal."

"Yea, but our Lord did forgive him. Can ye not forgive me, dear friend?"

"I can forgive, but justice must be done. How can I trust ye not to repeat your unspeakable behavior unless ye be punished for it?"

Though he pled with me as does a child found disobeying his parent, I was firm. At last, and to be rid of him, I promised to get the record extinguished if I could. With that assurance, such as it was, he departed.

When first he appeared in court, he was charged £20 to insure his appearance three months hence, and he was immediately expelled from the church. Though he had declared he loved me, I was unsurprised when the court found two other men, one from Plymouth and one from Barnstable, to testify to his unnatural behavior towards them. He denied his behavior with me (and I admit I felt a strange relief in his denial, as if it excluded me from his heinous touch) but admitted to the other charges.

William was stript of his position as constable at once. He was also crossed off the list of freemen, fined the £20 bond, and ordered to be put into the stocks. I suppose his former position as constable prevented his being whipt. If ever such charges were brought against him in the future, he was to be expelled from the colony. And if penetration had been--or would be in future--proved by two witnesses he would risk being hanged. Although the punishment seemed severe enough, it continued after the event, for he was cut off from the company of the community. Everyone shunned him.

He disappeared from the colony for a few years, and when he returned he purchased some land in Yarmouth and married the sister of Mrs. Matthew there. This was long after we had removed to Eastham and I rarely saw the man again. Whether he married for appearances or whether he had truly changed I neither know nor wish to know.

So there it be, my children. A sorry matter if ever there was one, yet I have my regrets about my part in it to this day. I pray God forgive me.

1644, THE DEATH OF STEPHEN HOPKINS, FROM THE MEMOIR OF GILES HOPKINS

WITHIN TWO YEARS of these events, your grandfather died after an illness that lasted but two months. Because he had told me what his will contained, I was not surprised to receive only a large bull from him. He had already given me a house when I married and many acres of land in Yarmouth out of his vast holdings. It disturbed me that he called in William Bradford and Myles Standish to witness his signing of the will and that Standish was its "supervisor." I guess he wanted the respectability these supposedly worthy men of Plymouth could supply. Also, I suspect, he knew they would be sure his wishes were carried out.

That Father called Caleb his "heir apparent" also disturbed me profoundly. Was it not enough Caleb received Father's house at Plymouth and all his land there, not to mention all the land due Father and a pair of oxen? Why was Caleb favored with such appellations as "heir apparent," "son and heir," "true and lawful Executor"? I do not mean to disparage your late uncle. I did love him. But I am writing a sort of confession now, and I must tell the truth. Should not his eldest son be appointed heir apparent?

Yet perhaps I have no right to complain. Did he not remember you, Stephen, my eldest son and his namesake? Did not he give my older sister, Constance, married to Nicholas Snow, his mare and only that? And certainly, because he was a father who cared more for his family than did many others care for theirs in the colony, even among the first comers, he did provide for his four other unmarried daughters, your aunts, Deborah, Damaris, Ruth, and Elizabeth, leaving them all the portable goods in his house, various cattle, and the right to live in his house while they were single. And, lovingly, he expressed his wish to be buried next to their mother, his late wife, Elizabeth.

In fine, I did miss him and do still for his many considerations, provisions, and disciplines, for his fatherly instruction and guidance. Yea, for his example and love. May he rest in peace.

13 FEBRUARY 1865, EASTHAM, CAPE COD

MY GOODNESS! DEAR reader, what have I been transcribing? I have peaked at what is coming. Is Aunt Huldah on to something? It seems as if our forefathers, or rather a goodly portion of them, could have resided in the Biblical cities of Sodom and Gomorrah. I fear to carry on, yet my curiosity will not let me stop. I see there is something here from Ruth, the half-sister of Giles and the younger sister of Caleb. Let me open the envelope. Why, it is a letter in her own hand. I must read this without hesitation.

C. 1646, LETTER FROM RUTH HOPKINS TO GILES HOPKINS

MY DEAR BROTHER Giles,

Methinks Father and Mother are turning over in their graves over what I have done. Not to mind, he is dead over a year now and she much longer and I can not speak their names, so Pequas tells me. Caleb will deliver this letter unto you if he can. I want ye to understand and know I have not died in the wilderness.

I write this in secret after the *Nickomo*, or winter feast, given by the father of Netop's mother. Her father was so kind to me, giving me new garments of deer skin and much purple wampum. As Pequas taught me, I thanked him three times and asked the gods to make him prosper. Everyone is asleep, so I take the opportunity to write.

There is no one to blame for what I have done. I used to listen to Netop's stories on Sabbath afternoons, hidden away so that ye could not know I was there. I begged Caleb to take me with him, away from the drudgery of my household chores and the lewd allurements of that man Mr. Hatch Father brought into the household. Ye know the man, full of entanglements and seductions, and I a girl not yet of age. Did ye not feel them yourself--not towards ye, but he filled the house with the odors of strange tropical flowers such as I have heard of, e'en though he slept in the store house.

At last Caleb did take me to see Netop's village, and there I met Pequas. She seemed to me more beautiful than the eagle, whose feather she wore in her hair and whose image is etched on her left arm. I thought her a handsome, brave warrior, not knowing till much later she was born a woman and after a vision became a man. I know not how to describe the influence of Pequas over me. It was as if I were another person, so powerful she was, so magical her manner. I felt my spirit one with hers.

Tonight she became the fox after which she is named and whose image she bears on her right arm. Her visage was covered by the head of a fox, and her hair, shaved on two sides but not in the middle, had three eagle feathers attached to the back. Around her neck and the top of her body were the pelts of the fox, and her naked belly was painted in white lines like lightning. Across her upper body and around her hips were plenty of wampum belts and she wore a leathern breech cloth and leather stockings, with wampum wrapt around them, and moccasins. In her right had she held a staff

175

with eagle feathers and fox tails; in her left was a tomahawk with feathers of I know not what kind. She was for a time the center of the dance as the others sang wonderful songs that I was told were about the hunt.

Pequas showed me the ways of the men, how they hunted deer by means of a fence made of brushwood in the shape of a V. The women and children watched on the side to keep the deer from jumping over the fence as the men persuaded the deer to run to the end of the trap. There they, Pequas among them, shot and killed them with their bows and arrows.

He, for that is what Pequas is called, hunts with the men, bringing back many fowl (turkeys, ducks, pigeons, &c.), fish (cod, haddock, salmon, sturgeon, &c.), and beasts (deer, beaver, raccoon, otter, and muskrat). If he brings a fox, he tells me he made a special prayer of thanksgiving for him. Pequas's first fox skin since I came to his village he gave to me.

In winter, I help prepare food with the other women. When we move the village during the planting season, I help in the fields. They gave me the job of using stone dibbles to make holes to plant the seed. It is almost fun because we talk (I am learning their language) and laugh at the hawks we have trained to keep the crows from eating our seed. The crows brought the seed to our people so we can not kill them. The boys help us keep the dogs and the wolves from eating our fish fertilizer until it rots in the earth.

The Indians, as ye must know, are not a dull people. Pequas does not do women's work. Like the men, she tends tobacco, but she never plants corn, beans, or squash as we women do. The life is not so hard as the English believe. We have a ceremony for almost every occasion to honor the spirits which provide the seeds and the crops. For tobacco, which as ye know has special powers, they stand in a circle before planting and offer leaves unto *Kiehtan*, always chanting prayers and singing. They burn it, the old crop, then they plant the new.

When my time of the month comes, I have rest in seclusion in my own little wigwam. Often I am joined by other women also in their monthly times, but no man, not even Pequas, can see us. The power of our female blood is too strong to risk mixing with it. Pequas has his own place to rest when necessary. There he receives some of his powwow visions. I miss him at these times, for I do love him, brother, as a woman loves her husband. And they have given me a new name: *Ottucke*, which they say means "little deer."

The mother and father of Pequas being dead, he invited me to live with him in his father's wigwam and help to bring up his younger brother and sisters. Sometimes he goes away to hunt or perform his duties as a powwow, as when he did help Netop to heal Caleb. I am sure you remember that. I thank God there is no war that Pequas must fight in now, though there has been talk of war with our ancient enemy, the Narragansetts. Massasoit is such a wise leader to have made peace with the English. Yet they are taking away the land of the Indians and they do not understand that this means they can not hunt on this land. They think the English mean to share it. I try to tell Pequas this, but he only says he will speak to our sachem.

So you see, dear brother, why I went away and what I am doing in the land of the Wampanoag. I beg you do not try to find me or take me away. I am very happy here and wish to stay. Please extend my love to my sisters.

Your most loving sister,
Ruth/Ottucke

13 FEBRUARY 1865, EASTHAM, CAPE COD

THIS IS AN astounding revelation! I see the envelope must not have come from Ruth. The name on it is not in her hand, and it seems it was sealed only once. I must be the first to open it since it was first sealed. What must Giles have thought of this? And what happened to Caleb? This is no ordinary family history. No wonder Giles (or whoever it was) sealed the envelope. I dare say he showed it to no one else. And yet, he was married to a half-Indian himself. It is past two o'clock in the morning, but I must continue. I must return to Giles's manuscript.

1644-54, FROM THE MEMOIR OF GILES HOPKINS

DEAR CHILDREN, FORGIVE the outburst against Caleb. I have no wish to be another Esau or Jacob for that matter. I have prayed God to forgive my resentment, and I fervently believe he has. Although subsequent events--but to those later.

Caleb was more generous to me than I deserved. Father was hardly laid in his grave when Caleb granted unto me and my heirs--that is, to you, my dear children--one hundred acres of land in Yarmouth. Shortly thereafter we removed to Eastham.

Unlike my friend John Cooke, for I suppose it is only right to call him my friend now, he still lives,--unlike him, I say, I readily took the Oath of Fidelity. I have been a surveyor of highways and served on juries. In short, I have tried to do my civic duties and be an example as a first comer, although only a child at the time, to this colony so many years ago.

That business with William Carsley, it has, I regret to tell you, followed me from time to time. In 1654 one William Leverish began to spread malicious lies about me, the nature of which ye may well imagine, he being an example of the depravity of spirit all men are born to yet few are redeemed from. I brought a suit of defamation against him and won, albeit I asked for £50 and he was fined just £20.

I FEAR I have been lacking as an example of a Christian father to some of you children. Only you can attest to my effectiveness in this matter. As ye know, I have always followed, like my parents, the Church of England, yet I have tolerated all other Christians, much like Roger Williams of Rhode Island, though I am not like him, a founder of colonies nor a missionary to the Indians as of late we have in seen in the persons of Daniel Gookin, John Eliot, Richard Bourne, and the Mayhews. Indeed, I am perhaps not a good example at all of a Christian to the Indians, for I never tried to convert them.

Yet I married a praying Indian--or the daughter of a praying Indian, Margaret Whelden, your grandmother, who became a godly woman, I believe, albeit she taught her children certain of the ways and beliefs of the Wampanoag people. Your grandfather too, Gabriel Whelden, did mend his ways and attended church regularly. Neither Gabriel nor his wife ever met the severe standards of the Separatists to become actual members of the church. I assured them God was no respecter of persons and if they truly believed in Christ our Lord, He would forgive them and receive them

179

into His arms when they passed from this earth. I believe I was correct.

Gabriel, like me, became a surveyor of highways. He too took the Oath of Fidelity and became a freeman. His son, Henry, volunteered to be a soldier against the Narragansetts, the ancient enemies of his mother's people, in 1645 but, as with the Pequots, the colony avoided war with the Narragansetts. Gabriel also attempted to prevent the marriage of your aunt Ruth, his daughter, to Richard Taylor because he doubted his character. Yet Gabriel relented before the court and gave his consent to the marriage. Some of the things I have to record here may be of interest to the surviving family of my wife. I give ye permission to show them these memoirs if you think it appropriate.

CHAPTER SEVEN
THE MEMOIR OF CATHERINE HOPKINS,
THE JOURNAL OF CALEB HOPKINS,
THE FURTHER HISTORY OF HER HUSBAND,
GILES HOPKINS,
&
THE END OF THE PLYMOUTH PAPERS

3 MARCH 1865, EASTHAM, CAPE COD

THESE RECENT REVELATIONS have given me pause to question what I am doing. Should I indeed be transcribing the papers I so innocently found in my aunt's attic? Should I finish my transcription and leave the papers for my ancestors to find? Or should I offer them to the public, suitably expurgated for the reader and for the privacy of my family? I suppose I will not have the answer to my questions until I have read and transcribed all of the papers. And, of course, I must confer with my brother and sister about what I ought to do. I have had no visits from our Aunt Huldah for two months, I am happy to report.

I am continually amazed by the content as well as the *authors* of these papers. For example, I never expected to find a memoir by the wife of Giles, Catherine Whelden Hopkins. Nevertheless, I present it here, transcribed as best as I can into modern English.

1677, THE MEMOIR OF CATHERINE WHELDEN HOPKINS

MY HUSBAND, TO whom I verily owe my ability to read and write, has prevailed upon me to write some few words about the history of my family, as he is doing, though he has not shown me yet what he has writ[ten]. I told him I durst not do it, for who would be interested in the history of a woman, and especially who would be interested in the history of the union of an Englishman and an Indian squaw? My gentle husband did calm my doubts. This memoir and his own, he did tell me, are meant not for the contemplation of the general public but for the benefit of our children, who may do with them as they please, even to the extent of showing them to others outside our family. Hence, I have agreed to write some few words. He counseled me that as a Christian woman I must tell the truth. I will essay to do just that.

My father, Gabriel Whelden, an Englishman, was not an acknowledged member of Plymouth Colony until the late 1630s, when I was myself but a young maid of about fifteen. My husband tells me he has recorded the events which led to my father coming to New England (with his brothers) and marrying my mother, the daughter of Quadequina, sachem of the Wampanoag and brother of the grand sachem, Massasoit. I knew neither of my father's brothers, but he and my mother did name their third child and first son, my brother Ralph, after the eldest of the two brothers. Mother trusted Gabriel that his brother Ralph was a good and Christian man.

In the matter of names, Mother, being more like the English than her own people, trusted Father entirely, even to the changing of her own name to Margaret, which was the name of his first wife in England. Mother said that changing names was a general practice among her people, and indeed among the English it is the practice for a woman to change her family name to that of her husband when she marries. I know her love for my father was so great that changing her name was a small matter.

For about ten years they lived among her people, as it is customary for a man to live with the people of his wife. I was brought up in both the Indian and the English ways. I learnt to plant the fields, to tend them, to prepare food for meals, to dismantle the wigwam for our seasonal movements, to gather wood for the fires, to dig for clams, capture lobster and fish, and to gather berries of all kinds (blueberries were my favorite when they could be found, we also had strawberries, cranberries, blackberries, elderberries, gooseberries, huckleberries, mulberries, raspberries, &c.; gathering berries was my favorite chore as a girl. I used to eat them till I was almost sick). Planting the fields required more labor, but the harvest was well worth our hard work.

As a woman, and especially as the daughter of the sachem, mother was not excluded from the business of the people. She met with the other women and their opinions were considered. Father also was included in the councils of the men, though I believe from my early years he wished to return to the life of an Englishman or, rather, to become a colonist in good standing. He and some of the other men would, from time to time, help the women in the fields. They were solely responsible for the growing of the sacred tobacco.

When I say "sacred," I should explain, since I am writing for my children (and others who might not understand), that in truth everything was sacred to the Indians. If not sacred, then everything had a spiritual meaning to them. They did not separate themselves from the natural world. For almost any activity (besides games and joking, of which there is far more than the English realize) they have a ceremony, even if it is just a prayer, to honor the spirit of the animal, the plant, the sun, moon, stars, sky, earth, islands, streams, rivers, and the sea. We are all part of each other. We are the People of the Dawn, and our responsibility was to assure the right balance in nature.

When the men burnt the meadows and cut trees, it was to make hunting or planting more easy or to make canoes. We had no need for fences to protect our land. The sachem might have assigned certain lands to plow to certain families, but no one was harmed if he hunted around that land. And no one went hungry. If a person were too deformed or old to work, that person was fed and taken care of by his family or the people if the man or woman, boy or girl, had no family. I remember only one or two examples of such a person without a family. We are very loyal to our kin.

It is true we women had to skin the animals our men hunted and to make the garments they wore and we and the children wore. We had to pluck the wild turkey, ducks, &c., and otherwise prepare them to eat. Do not the English women do the same? They do buy their pots and kitchen ware from England, and so do we. Some of our older women continue to craft pots and weave baskets, and the men make pipes and wampum, yet there were women who made wampum and bows and arrows as well. Generally, we women had charge of the house; the men had charge of hunting, growing tobacco, and protecting the village.

When an Indian woman has a baby, the birth is generally easy compared to the birth of English children. This I have observed. The babe is put on a bed of duck down, moss, milkweed down or cattails--whatever is at hand. The father builds a flat cradleboard smoothed over for the baby to be strapped on. The mother returns to her duties directly. She will set her babe down near her as she works, weeding the fields and gardens &c. and carry it home when finished with her work. As we lived among the English in

Mattacheese (or Yarmouth, as the English call it), I quit the custom of using a cradleboard. Each of you, my children, gave me no trouble in birth, apart from John, but that is no matter. I loved you all.

C. 1646-1676, RALPH WHELDEN AND SQUANNIT, FROM THE MEMOIR OF CATHERINE HOPKINS

MY HUSBAND TELLS me I should inform ye about your uncle, Ralph, he who was named after my father's brother in England. None of ye, I think, ever met him. We always told you he preferred to live with the Indians. We have never explained the reasons. This part of the story should stay within the family or the English, should they find out, would kill or sell into slavery all those like the one Ralph took into his wigwam. The Indian word for their house, you may remember, is *wetu*.

This person Ralph fell in love with was called Squannit, after a famous grandmother in the legends of the Wampanoag. That was not the person's birth name. I do not remember what that was if ever I knew it. Squannit was born a boy. Perchance to help you understand, children, I should tell you some little stories to explain people like Squannit who have traits, or humors, characteristic of both sexes. One story says that a woman had twins in her but *Kiehtan* decided to make them into one child, both a boy and a girl. The child was thus born with two spirits. Another tells the story of the giant, Maushop. Although he was married to Squant, he fell for the Wild Cat and wished to dally with him. To do this, Maushop donned women's clothes and seduced the Wild Cat. After nine months Maushop pretended to have a child. This did not fool Wild Cat, so Maushop revealed himself as a man and flew to his island home. The Indians say Maushop thus announced the coming of the men-women, people like Squannit.

Pequas, the woman warrior and powwow your aunt Ruth went to live with, was like Squannit, only he was born a woman. The Wampanoag people believe you are what the Great Spirit made you, and you can not avoid your destiny. From the time they were little children barely able to walk, Squannit was drawn to women's things--pots, seed planting, weaving baskets. Pequas, on the other hand, was drawn to men's things--tomahawks, bows and arrows, and tobacco pipes. Only when they each had their own spirit vision did the people fully accept them as the two-spirited people they are. Yes, the English if they knew would hang them or whip and brand them, perhaps sell them into slavery. That is why the Indians have never revealed unto the leaders of the colony, and the other colonists, the existence of these kinds of people among them. My father was different because for a time he became an Indian. So far as I know, Mother never told him what he should do, with this one exception. He must keep the secret of the existence of these men-women and women-men always. He did and so should you.

Being raised among the Indians, I never had the prejudice against such people the Separatists and, indeed, the Anglicans had, though I converted to the Church of England long ago. I remember rumors, told me by my father, that King James himself was a man who loved men, even though of course he married a woman to produce an heir to the throne, as was his duty. It makes no matter now, for I write of things in the long ago past.

The ordinary European visitor, such as your father or his father, would not have been likely to have noticed that Pequas was born a woman or Squannit a man. Most probably they thought Pequas a man and Squannit a woman. Pequas always dressed as a man and Squannit as a woman, with shiny black hair down to her waist. Her mantle was like that of a woman, only it always covered her breasts, unlike the other women who often went without a mantle in summer. She wore a long shirt and women's leggings, much shorter than the men's, coming up just under the knees. And she generally wore wampum, though not when she worked in the fields. They each performed the tasks assigned to a man or a woman, withal Squannit knew how to fight with a club and could do battle and, I believe did when she was killed in the recent war with Metacom.

Indian men and women are very modest about the sexual function, and they never kiss or hold hands or show such other affections as occur between men and women, except in private. I am certain no English women were molested in the war with Metacom. Indians do not do that sort of thing, unlike the English. Generally, both Indian and English are very modest about touching their loved ones or otherwise showing carnal desire in public. Indians differ from the English when it comes to dalliance before marriage. The Indians care not about such things, whereas the English become hysterical about them and devise all manner of punishments for those who practice them or whom they imagine guilty of such practices. Marriage is a different matter for the Indians. No dalliance with others after marriage!

Pequas and Squannit were very comely, and I am sure Ruth and Ralph were first attracted by their beauty. They were also tender-hearted, hard working, loving spouses. Squannit was very good with children, very patient and gentle. Ralph came to marry another woman, a born woman, as is the custom for important people among the Indians. He was accepted as a member of the sachem's council and therefore was important to the village. Both wives lived in the same *wetu* with Ralph and raised his children.

Your father was not so understanding as was I. He had not the advantage of my upbringing among the Indians. But I will allow him to tell his story. I hope what I have written suffices.

21 MARCH 1865, EASTHAM, CAPE COD

GOOD HEAVEN'S SAKE'S alive! My ancestors were perverted. Why am I writing this? Why do I write, "dear reader," when I doubt there will be a reader? "Leviticus . . . the Apostle Paul." Dear Aunt Huldah, why did I not listen to you—heed your deathbed warning? I dare not appear even to countenance such--I know not what to call it--such wickedness, misconduct, wrongdoing, ought I use the word, "sin"?--to see the light of day. Yet, I must know the truth. Surely, as Catherine hints, Giles put a stop to this indecent behavior. Let me see.

What is this I find? A few well-weathered leaves of parchment, written in a strange hand with many blots on the paper. Who could have authored this? What name concludes this set of antique vellum? *Caleb.* Yes, that name which I have been pursuing throughout these papers from Plymouth.

But this is not from Plymouth. *Barbadoes.* Ah, Barbados, the British colony in the far-eastern part of the Caribbean Islands. Did I not read something about it in Gov. Bradford's history? "Their son became a seaman & dyed at Barbadoes. . . ." That would be my Caleb. What happened that he became a sailor and died on Barbados? Perhaps these pages will tell.

1651, THE JOURNAL OF CALEB HOPKINS

I AM SICK with a fatal malady, I fear, yet there is no reason for me to make a will. I gave all I had to give before I set out to sea. When was that? Three, four, five years ago? Memory fails. My brother Giles forced me to do it, to become a sailor. It was either that or die in the wilderness among my people, the native inhabitants of the New World. Long ago I forgave him or, rather, I surrendered my anger, which ate at me and threatened to kill me as certainly as this tropical fever threatens to do. No balance. Oh for a powwow. Netop or Pequas. To heal this foreign sickness. How did it come to this?

To blame anyone now is useless, futile. My earliest memory: a tiny, overcrowded room, fire burning in the corner. Mother singing softly, rocking my sister Deborah, or was it Damaris, in her arms. No one else in the house. They all had work to do. Work, work, work. That was the lot of life then and ever afterwards, but for happy spells listening to Netop tell stories, and then my life in what Giles called the wilderness. Why that? It was no wilderness to me. By then I knew every Indian trail, every Indian skill to live in harmony there, rather like the harmonious strains of Mother's songs. She did teach us to sing with her in harmony, as later the ones I came to own as my people did also. To the English ear their tones were harsh and out of tune. Barbaric they were called--not by my father or mother, nay, certainly not by my brother but by the others in the English village. I heard the Indian voices speak to my soul. Even now they sing there. *Noe wammaw ause. Noe wammaw ause,* he sang to me.

"Rather old to be starting out as a sailor," I was told.
I was a quick learner. "My father, I said, had been at sea."
True, but he was no sailor. I have now seen more than he on
his journeys to Bermuda, Virginia, back to England, then to
Plymouth. I've been to all those places and more--Maine,
Nova Scotia, Norway, Holland, the West Indies on fishing
pinnaces and larger vessels. Not an easy life, but one that
took me away, far away from the troubles I never myself
created. And then I signed on to this last abominable voyage,
not knowing how truly wicked it was.

This place is as different as night is from day
compared to my homeland. Here there is only one season--
endless days of warm, balmy weather, whiskery fig trees,
guava, cassava, cotton, peanuts, corn, palms, fragrant tropical
flowers. The sugar cane is replacing tobacco as the crop of
choice which we seaman have to transport, and what I find so
odious is the cycle we English help propel: from Boston
come black slaves stolen in Africa or purchased from their
fellow Africans. These are brought here and sold for
tobacco, sugar, &c. They have some white indentured
servants, but more and more the laborers the planters use are
black slaves. I am told it was the Dutch and the Spanish and
Portuguese Jewish merchants who pressed for this exchange.
On some of the other islands I have seen Pequots from New
England sold by the Puritans after the Pequot War. There are
very few of them. They die quickly in this strange new world.

The English here like to boast of their House of
Assembly, which they started in 1639, twelve years after
Captain Henry Powell came to settle the island with 80
settlers and 10 slaves. They say it is a parliament much like
that in England, but of course only freemen may vote there.
Although the number of slaves is not large, I can not help but

feel responsible, even though I have no control over any of this business in my job as master mate, and I was going to quit that slave ship and return to a fishing ship. I have heard there was once a native population on this island but slavery and European diseases killed them off.[1] It is a familiar and monstrous tale. Am I dying because of my part in this? I pray God forgive me.

I NEVER ASKED Father to name me "heir apparent" in his last will and testament. Perhaps Mother influenced him, though she herself had long before gone to be with God. Perhaps Father meant to keep me at home, make me a farmer. That I was never meant to be. From my youngest years I wanted nothing more than to live with the Indians. Work was tedious, church was tedious, only those Sabbath sessions with Netop, Mawpaw, and my brother made my week bearable. I would repeat in my head the stories and long for the Sabbath to arrive so I could hear a new one. I thought Giles understood this and felt as I felt. When I was sick unto death, he called Netop and Pequas to heal me after no one in the village could help.

From that time onward my one purpose was to join the Indians, and especially to live with Netop and Mawpaw, for I loved them as David did love Jonathan. Yet instead of improving, English relations with the Indians decayed like the fertilizer fish we planted after their fashion in our fields. When after Father died Ruth begged me to take her to

---

[1] My research reveals that when the English arrived, Barbados was uninhabited. Arawak Indians from South America had inhabited the island, but they disappeared for unknown reasons in the 16th century (Gary A. Puckrein, *Little England: Plantation Society and Anglo-Barbadian Politics, 1627-1700*). (Brandon Taylor)

Netop's village, I realized the power of the Great Spirit we call God and the Indians call *Manitou* (and sometimes *Kiehtan* or *Cauta'ntouwit*) was beckoning me to join our Indian brothers and sisters and, yea, become one of them.

Netop said I was too old to go through the ordeals he had gone through to become a man. What I could and did do was fast all alone for four days without food or water in an isolated place in the woods until I had a vision of myself as an Indian lover and man. By the end of the first day I had lost control of my senses. I saw a great eagle descending from the night sky. The stars were as bright as the sun. The eagle came and placed his beak upon my nose and stared straight into mine eyes. An overwhelming feeling of love and oneness wrapt me up in the eagle's wings. When I came back to the present world, I found Netop and Mawpaw standing there. They told me four days were gone. I had no idea so much time had passed. I felt one with Netop and Mawpaw.

Squannit gave me a new, secret name. My public name was Wobsacuck, meaning "eagle." And that is who I am to this day, though no one calls me Wobsacuck. The spirit of the eagle guides me. I have his image tattooed over my heart. Nobody taunts me about it. Sailors are expected to have tattoos.

When I left Plymouth to live with the Indians, I promised my sisters to return. Neighbors, members of the grand jury and such, watched me, so I left at night. I knew the path. And I did return from time to time. Ruth continued to beg me to take her with me and I did. Her sister Elizabeth had gone to live with Richard and Pandora Sparrow, and Deborah and Damaris were set to marry. In truth, I had no responsibilities after I gave the house to Giles.

Mawpaw had become a majestical man--taller than I am, limbs of a warrior, brave brown skin, a nape that made me shiver and slide down his spine into his very own life of membrane, tissue, & muscle, a face I melted into, eyes as deep as the blood of his people. I lived with him and Netop, who had married and had two little children.

No English person, apart from my sister-in-law, wife of Giles, who is herself half Indian, will understand my love of the Indians or my love for Mawpaw. We loved each other as husband and wife, save we were equals. We were both men, not men-women like Squannit. The Indians neither encouraged our love nor frowned upon it. "You are *Manitou*," they would say.

Oh how short our time together was! I had never known such happiness as I had with Mawpaw. After our first love making, we built our own *wetu* and lived in it together. We pledged our own solemn oath of fidelity to each other. The English did not like a man to live alone, and they pressed such a man to obtain permission to live for himself. Two men living together were pressed to do the same and forever looked upon with suspicion. The neighbors would watch them to force them to live according to the English notion of propriety. The Indians were not like this at all. They knew love when they saw it and they saw it in us. They cared not as long as we did our duties as men of the village.

The light is fading. I can barely hold this pen. I leave these words as testimony that others may fare better in some distant future. Soon I will join my lover in the after world, in the Southwest, the land of the Great Spirit. Bury me facing that way with my tomahawk and wampum.

And, dear friend Trevor, take these papers to my family. My brother will know who you are.

[Signed]

Caleb Hopkins
Barbadoes,
15 March 1651

8 APRIL 1865, EASTHAM, CAPE COD

WHAT A PITIFUL, ghastly, lurid tale. My body feels
empty, like a bucket whose dirty laundry water has been
thrown to the grass. Have I inherited such sodomitical
tendencies in my blood? Is that why I have never felt
compelled to love another woman in the manner necessary to
marry her? Horrors! What would have become of *me* had I
lived in those times? What became of Caleb's Indian
consort? These few pages that remain of Giles's manuscript
must finish this tale.

22 AUGUST 1677, THE MEMOIR OF GILES HOPKINS

AND NOW, MY children, I come to the hardest part of
this history. You know I did not participate in the war
against King Philip that has destroyed forever, I fear, our
peaceful relationships with the Indians. Indeed, I fear the war
has destroyed the native inhabitants and original owners of
this country forever. Although I did not fight in that war, I
am guilty of far greater sin. I write this to purge my soul and
to leave you a record for the future after I am gone.

I had left our father's house and property in Caleb's
hands when he conveyed them to me after our father died. I
made sure Elizabeth, my youngest sister, was indentured to
Richard and Pandora Sparrow. Deborah was spoken for by
Andrew Ring and Damaris by Jacob Cooke, brother of my
old friend, John Cooke.

Caleb, always a restless spirit, was frequently absent, but we had an indentured servant, Jeremiah Foyle, to look after the property and protect the women. And Richard Sparrow lived nearby. I had not an inkling how long were the periods Caleb was gone nor that Ruth had joined him till I went to visit Plymouth in the late spring of 1646. Then Deborah handed me a letter from Ruth that told me she had joined Caleb and that she had formed a--I know not how to call it--a grotesque bond with Pequas, of all people. Ruth called Pequas a she, then called her a he. What else had he or she been all those years? I was in the dark. My sister had become an Indian, it appeared, as my father-in-law had once done. She knew I was not the man to judge her, having myself married a half-Indian woman. Yet we are Christians. Ruth had forsaken the church.

I made preparations to find her and discover the nature of this nonsense and what Caleb was doing. My wife asked me also to find her brother Ralph if I could. He too had disappeared.

Richard Sparrow agreed to join me, and we set off a week later just at the start of planting time. We traveled directly to Netop's village along Indian paths familiar to me.

Netop welcomed us with muskrat stew, some parched corn, and a pipe of tobacco. After we had conversed for a short time I came to the point.

"Have ye seen my brother Caleb and my sister Ruth?"

"Yea, they be living in this village," Netop said. "Ruth is out on the hill planting seed. Caleb and Mawpaw are hunting."

Remembering my wife's request, I asked after Ralph too.

Netop never changed his expression. "Ralph lives here with Squannit."

"I don't think I know Squannit."

"She has lived in the village for many years. I will bring you to her if you wish. She is in their *wetu* now."

"And are they married?"

Netop only nodded. "What of Ruth and Pequas?" He nodded again, never changing his stoic expression.

Although I thought I knew Netop well, I was not a little distraught by his behaving very much like an Indian, not as the friend I knew on Sabbath afternoons.

I guessed why his behavior was so different when late in the afternoon I saw Caleb, Mawpaw, Ralph, Pequas and two or three other men returning from the hunt, all of them in the Indian garb, wearing leathern breeches, leggings, and moccasins. Their skin was well oiled. Seeing them from a distance, anyone would have taken Caleb and Ralph for Indians. The hunting party carried a middling-sized deer and a few rabbits.

Caleb greeted me in a more than usually hardy fashion.

"Brother!" he said. "Welcome! You know Mawpaw, do you not?"

We shook hands in English fashion, as I did with the others.

"You must come to our *wetu* and sup," said Caleb. I was confounded when I discovered he meant a wigwam he shared with Mawpaw and only Mawpaw. Yet I had no time to contemplate this discovery because Ruth came at that time. She did run to me and put her arms around me and said, "How good to see you, brother! Did ye receive my letter?" I said I had. "I hope ye be not angry with me. I am very

196

happy here." She looked at Pequas, who gave the barest suggestion of a smile.

"Well, I suppose you are old enough to decide for yourself now. If Caleb agrees with your living arrangements here, I do not object."

"I do," said Caleb.

NOW THINGS BEGAN to happen so quickly I have had to think hard to remember them. After they washed themselves in the river, Richard and I joined Caleb and Mawpaw in their *wetu*. It looked like an ordinary Wampanoag wigwam. There was a pot over the fire, and in it Mawpaw had put meat from a deer that had already been slain by him and prepared by Ruth, so he said.

We sat, the four of us, smoking a pipe and waiting for Ruth and Pequas to come. I had brought my musket and a knife, as had Richard. The muskets we placed on the floor. The knives were sheathed by our sides.

Caleb sat inordinately close to Mawpaw. I thought little of it till I noticed Caleb had his arm around him. The tobacco smoke had altered my mind, for I was not used to it, and I saw an apparition, I thought, of the two of them looking into each other's visage as lovers do. I looked at Richard, and he bore a strange and disapproving look, as if he were seeing what I saw. My face burned with shame and anger.

"Giles," I heard a voice like that of Caleb say. "How do you like our little house?"

I do not know what possessed me at that moment, but faster than a snake, I had my knife in my hand and I stabbed Mawpaw in the heart. Confusion reigned. The next thing I knew Ruth and Pequas were in the wigwam and

Pequas had hold of me with a knife, *my knife*, to my throat. Caleb had grabbed Richard, and Ruth was holding his knife. "Go for Netop," Caleb shouted. "Quickly!"

NETOP RETURNED WITH Ruth, but it was too late to help Mawpaw. My one stab had wounded him mortally. The cry from Caleb I will not forget till the day I die. He wept and cried aloud for I know not how long. Netop and the others took me and Richard and secured us to two trees. I am sure had Netop not been my old friend, they would have killed us then and there.

Yet perhaps not. We were Englishmen from Plymouth, and killing us would have caused great enmity between the Indians and the colony. It would have exposed their lascivious and unnatural practices. We were kept there, bound, all through the preparations for the burial of Mawpaw. Pequas dug his grave and, as was their custom, they built planks and made something like a coffin in the hole. They placed him there on a mat, facing the Southwest in the position of a baby. Then they covered him with his things--his knife, bows and arrows, hatchet, a bowl of parched corn, and much wampum. They howled like wolves and the men cried along with the women. I was too weak from lack of sleep and bondage to cry or do anything but watch as they placed his sleeping mat on Mawpaw and covered his grave with the dirt that Pequas had dug. Then more moaning and mourning.

After two or three days, Caleb spoke to me. "Brother Giles, they want to torture you and kill you and Richard. But Netop and I have counseled against it. We will let you return to your homes if you give your solemn word you will never reveal what you have seen here and if you promise never to harm an Indian again."

WE GAVE OUR word and we were set free. I told Caleb he should consider leaving that country for a time. I never saw him again, and I wish to God I had begged his forgiveness. The best I can do is write this, for I have begged forgiveness from our Lord and Savior many times.

After he had sailed to England as a seaman, Caleb sent a letter to let me know what he had done. I told my wife and my sisters and Governor Bradford that he had gone to sea, but we never heard from Caleb again until a message came from him written in Barbados just before he died of a fever there. I thought I knew the man who brought the message, but he said nothing except he was a fellow sailor with Caleb.

By then I had named my next boy child after him. Ruth lived long after Caleb, and as ye know Catherine and I named our next daughter after her. Caleb and Ruth, be ye proud of your uncle and aunt whose names you bare. They followed where their hearts did lead them. Who am I, who have done the same, to judge them? I leave judgement to God who alone knows the human heart.

Catherine and her brother Henry went and visited Ralph and Ruth. I could not show my face in that village again. Ralph received Catherine and Henry gladly, and she saw him and Ruth again a few times before the great war with King Philip started. I believe Ralph and Squannit and Ruth and Pequas perished in that war.

Forgive me Catherine that I never told you of my true guilt in Mawpaw's death nor the true reasons Caleb left to become a seaman. Now you know the truth and, God willing, you will forgive me as I believe He has forgiven me.

[Signed]

Giles Hopkins

EASTHAM, CAPE COD
20 APRIL 1865

MY DEAR GOD, I never anticipated such a gruesome and sorrowful conclusion to these memoirs. They can not be published without such expurgations as would make the story incomprehensible--unless I should embellish the tale. No, that would be dishonest. That would be wrong. I can not do it.

Was Aunt Huldah right? She wanted me to destroy these papers with their horrible revelations. That I can not do. I never said I would. As my ancestor, Giles Hopkins, declares, who am I to judge? Yet I have my scruples and my reputation to consider, not to mention my dear, sweet nephew, Paul.

I will leave these revelations secret, hidden away, even from James and Sarah, as I found them, like the terrible things Young Goodman Brown learned on that awful night he tempted fate and left his bride, Faith, at home with her pink ribbons or the dreadful secrets kept in his heart by the minister with the black veil. They shall keep, safely guarded in this ancient family chest, until a better day has dawned. When that day may arrive I do not know, certainly not in my lifetime.

I HESITATE EVEN to write my name here, though future generations of my family surely will know it. The horrific war that tore our country apart is over at last. The slaves are free, the union saved, and I fear the federal troops will now be sent to finish off whatever Indians are left in the West.

The nation has had little time to celebrate its victory, for, tragically, the president was assassinated on Good Friday within days after the war ended by one whose name deserves not to be written. Oh, what will the future hold? I dare not speculate.

I, BRANDON TAYLOR, husband of Alberto Tovar and descendant of Caleb Taylor through his nephew, Paul, and of the *Mayflower* Hopkins family, do hereby bring these *Plymouth Papers* to the public in the dawn of the better day Caleb Taylor spoke of. The fates of the main characters in this novel, as far as they are known, are as follows:

GILES HOPKINS lived much longer than he expected. He wrote a will in Eastham, Cape Cod, dated 19 January 1682, and added a codicil on 5 March 1689. He died some time between that date and the date of probate for the will, 16 April 1690, at the age of about 82.

CATHERINE HOPKINS, who is mentioned as "Catorne" in Giles's will (and whose name is also spelled Katherne), died some time after 5 March 1689.

CALEB HOPKINS, son of Stephen Hopkins, was buried by his brother in Barbados, late March 1651, age 28.

RUTH HOPKINS, daughter of Stephen Hopkins, lived on with PEQUAS among the Wampanoags until the time of King Philip's War, 1675-76, as did RALPH and SQUANNIT. The dates of their deaths are unknown.

NETOP lived with his wife and children practicing his healing powers as a powwow and serving from time to time as an emissary from his people to the English until the time of King Philip's War. The date of his death is unknown.

CALEB TAYLOR lived to the age of 75 and died in his sleep in Boston, 1889, without ever having published the *Plymouth Papers* and without revealing their full contents to anyone except his nephew, **PAUL**, who married at the age of 30, had one child, a son, and died in the year 1919, at the age of 71.

--Long Beach, California
6 January 2014

ACKNOWLEDGMENTS

First, I want to thank my 3rd cousin, Robert C. Snyder, a better genealogist than I, who informed me in an email dated 17 April 2003 that another genealogist had informed him that we are descended from three *Mayflower* families, those of Stephen Hopkins, Francis Cooke, and Richard Warren. I was skeptical at first because we had no tradition of *Mayflower* ancestry whatsoever in my family. *The Plymouth Papers* really began when I got this news from Bob Snyder. With his help and that of other cousins who do family history and with the help of the Mayflower Society, I was able to garner enough evidence to be accepted as a member of that Society in September 2005--sufficient to make me believe I am a descendant of the above *Mayflower* passengers. *The Plymouth Papers* is, of course, a work of fiction, part historical fact, part invention--what could well have happened.

Indispensable for my family history research and subsequently this novel was a trip during the first week of April 2004 to Plymouth, Massachusetts, where I was able to gather information about and from the original sites of the colony. My visit to the reconstructed colony as it was in 1627, Plimoth Plantation, on 6 April 2004 (and to the *Mayflower II* on the following day) was invaluable for an understanding not only of the layout of Plymouth in 1627 but also of the living conditions then of both the Plymouth settlers and the Wampanoags and of those on the *Mayflower* itself.

The following sources have also been useful in my research for and writing of *The Plymouth Papers*. I list them roughly in the order I use them in the novel: William Bradford, *Of Plymouth Plantation, 1620-1647*, ed. Samuel Eliot

Morison; Samuel Purchas, *Purchas His Pilgrimage*; *Mourt's Relation: A Journal of the Pilgrims at Plymouth*, ed. Dwight B. Heath; *Records of the Colony of New Plymouth in New England*, ed. Nathaniel B. Shurtleff and David Pulsifer, 12 volumes; John D. Austin, *Mayflower Families Through Five Generations*, Vol. 6, 3rd edition, Stephen Hopkins; Ralph V. Wood, Jr., *Mayflower Families Through Five Generations*, Vol. 12, Francis Cooke; Eugene Aubrey Stratton, *Plymouth Colony: Its History and People, 1620-1691*; Caleb Johnson, "The True Origin of Stephen Hopkins of the *Mayflower*," *The American Genealogist*, Vol. 73, No. 3, 1998; Margaret Hodges, *Hopkins of the Mayflower: Portrait of a Dissenter*; the Rheims New Testament, 1582; the Geneva Bible (1611 edition), the Bible used by the Separatists on the *Mayflower;* the Authorized King James Version of the Bible; Walt Whitman's *Complete Poems and Selected Prose*, ed. James E. Miller, Jr.; *The Portable Hawthorne*, ed. Malcom Cowley; Bruce C. Daniels, *Puritans at Play: Leisure and Recreation in Colonial New England*; James Deetz and Patricia Scott Deetz, *The Times of Their Lives: Life, Love, and Death in Plymouth Colony*; Cheryl Harness, *Three Young Pilgrims*; Daniel Gookin, *Historical Collections of the Indians and Historical Account of the Doings and Sufferings of the Christian Indians in New England in the Years 1675-1677*; Edward Winslow, *Good News from New England*; Roger Williams, *A Key to the Language of America* (indispensable for this project); William Wood, *New England's Prospect*, ed. Alden T. Vaughan; Ronald Dale Karr, *Indian New England, 1524-1674*; John Pory, Emmanuel Altham, and Isaack de Rasieres, *Three Visitors to Early Plymouth*, ed. Sydney V. James, Jr.; Howard S. Russell, *Indian New England Before the Mayflower*; Alden T. Vaughan, *New England Frontier: Puritans and Indians, 1620-1675*; C. Keith Wilbur, *The New England Indians*, 2nd ed.; Catherine Marten, *The Wampanoags in the*

Seventeenth Century; Neal Salisbury, *Manitou and Providence: Indians, Europeans, and the Making of New England, 1500-1643*; Kathleen J. Bragdon, *Native People of Southern New England, 1500-1650*; Ann Marie Plane, *Colonial Intimacies: Indian Marriage in Early New England*.

Other sources I found useful on Native American queer history are Will Roscoe's *Changing Ones: Third and Fourth Genders in Native America* and Sabine Lang's *Men as Women, Women as Men: Changing Gender in Native American Cultures*, trans. John L. Vantine. I also used and recommend John (Fire) Lame Deer and Richard Erdoes's *Lame Deer, Seeker of Visions*. The marriage of Giles Hopkins to a half-Wampanoag Indian is based on oral histories by Franklyn Bearce, Ele-wath-thum or Swimming Eel, deposited at the Library of Congress and at the New York Public Library.

Other sources I used are the following: "A Dash of Cape Cod," *Putnam's Magazine* 9.49 (1857); *1621: A New Look at Thanksgiving*, published by the National Geographic Society in cooperation with Plimoth Plantation; "Landing of the Pilgrims," *The Ladies' Repository* 18.1 (1858); William S. Simmons, *Spirit of the New England Tribes*; Mary Rowlandson, *A True History of the Captivity and Restoration of Mrs. Mary Rowlandson*; Jill Grossman, *Revelations of New England Architecture: People and their Buildings*; Milton Meltzer, *Slavery: A World History*; H. Roger King, *Cape Cod and Plymouth Colony in the Seventeenth Century*; "Eastham Camp Meeting," *Gleason's Pictorial Magazine* 1.20 (1851); www.barbados.org and www.bbc.co.uk/history; and, finally, John Demos, *A Little Commonwealth: Family Life in Plymouth Colony*.

I am grateful to Michael A. Knight and the Helene Wurlitzer Foundation of New Mexico, where, on a residence fellowship, I wrote the first draft of *The Plymouth Papers*.

Without that support and Ann Brantingham's generous faith in my work, this little novel would never have seen the light of the world outside my computer files. I owe a huge thank you to John Brantingham for reading the manuscript and offering invaluable suggestions. As always, thanks to my partner in life, Mario Hernandez, for his patience, understanding, and love.

--Clifton Snider
6 January 2014

ABOUT THE AUTHOR

Photo courtesy of Deborah Snider

Clifton Snider, faculty emeritus at California State University, Long Beach, is the internationally celebrated author of ten books of poetry. A career retrospective of his work, *Moonman: New and Selected Poems*, was published to great acclaim by World Parade Books (2012). He has published three previous novels: *Loud Whisper* (2000), *Bare Roots* (2001), and *Wrestling with Angels: A Tale of Two Brothers* (2001). As a Jungian/Queer literary critic, he has published numerous articles and a book, *The Stuff That Dreams Are Made On* (1991), on Victorian and 20th-century authors, as well as the story and film adaptation of *Brokeback Mountain*. His work has been translated into Arabic, French, Russian, and Spanish.

www.ingramcontent.com/pod-product-compliance
Lightning Source LLC
Chambersburg PA
CBHW020632250626
47154CB00008B/2644

* 9 7 8 0 6 1 5 9 5 6 9 1 6 *